THE COLOSSUS

A NOVEL

OPIE READ

1st WORLD
LIBRARY
Literary Society

The Colossus

Opie Read

© 1st World Library, 2008
PO Box 2211
Fairfield, IA 52556
www.1stworldlibrary.com
First Edition

LCCN: 2007935408

Softcover ISBN: 978-1-4218-9358-7
Hardcover ISBN: 978-1-4218-9458-4
eBook ISBN: 978-1-4218-9258-0

Purchase *"The Colossus"*
as a traditional bound book at:
www.1stWorldLibrary.com/purchase.asp?ISBN=978-1-4218-9358-7

1st World Library is a literary, educational organization
dedicated to:

- Creating a free internet library of downloadable ebooks

- Hosting writing competitions and offering book publishing
  scholarships.

Interested in more 1st World Library books? contact:
literacy@1stworldlibrary.com
Check us out at: www.1stworldlibrary.com

1st World Library Literary Society

Giving Back to the World

"If you want to work on the core problem, it's early school literacy."

- James Barksdale, former CEO of Netscape

"No skill is more crucial to the future of a child, or to a democratic and prosperous society, than literacy."

- Los Angeles Times

"Literacy... means far more than learning how to read and write... The aim is to transmit... knowledge and promote social participation."

- UNESCO

"Literacy is not a luxury, it is a right and a responsibility. If our world is to meet the challenges of the twenty-first century we must harness the energy and creativity of all our citizens."

- President Bill Clinton

"Parents should be encouraged to read to their children, and teachers should be equipped with all available techniques for teaching literacy, so the varying needs and capacities of individual kids can be taken into account."

- Hugh Mackay

CONTENTS

I. LOOKING BACK AT EARLY LIFE 9

II. A SLEEPY VILLAGE AND A FUSSY OLD MAN 15

III. ALL WAS DARKNESS 20

IV. A STRANGE REQUEST 28

V. DISSECTING A MOTIVE 36

VI. WAITING AT THE STATION 39

VII. A MOTHER'S AFFECTION...............................48

VIII. THE DOMAIN OF A GREAT MERCHANT 51

IX. THE INTERVIEWERS 67

X. ROMPED WITH THE GIRL.................................76

XI. ACKNOWLEDGED BY SOCIETY 85

XII. A DEMOCRACY..88

XIII. BUTTING AGAINST A WALL.............................. 104

XIV. A DIFFERENT HANDWRITING............................ 111

XV. TOLD HIM HER STORY............................... 117

XVI. AN AROUSER OF THE SLEEPY 123

XVII. AN OLD MAN WOULD INVEST 133

XVIII. THE INVESTMENT.................................... 141

XIX. ARRESTED EVERYWHERE............................... 144

XX. CRIED A SENSATION 157

XXI. A HELPLESS OLD WOMAN 163

XXII. TO GO ON A VISIT 170

XXIII. HENRY'S INCONSISTENCY 175

XXIV. WORE A ROSE ON HIS COAT 180

XXV. IMPATIENTLY WAITING 189

XXVI. TOLD IT ALL 196

XXVII. POINTS OUT HER BROTHER'S DUTY 205

XXVIII. THE VERDICT 214

XXIX. A DAY OF REST 222

XXX. A MOTHER'S REQUEST 228

XXXI. A MOMENT OF ARROGANCE 237

XXXII. A MOST PECULIAR FELLOW 251

XXXIII. THE TIME WAS DRAWING NEAR 257

XXXIV. TOLD HIM A STORY 266

XXXV. CONCLUSION 273

CHAPTER I

LOOKING BACK AT EARLY LIFE

When the slow years of youth were gone and the hastening time of manhood had come, the first thing that Henry DeGolyer, looking back, could call from a mysterious darkness into the dawn of memory was that he awoke one night in the cold arms of his dead mother. That was in New Orleans. The boy's father had aspired to put the face of man upon lasting canvas, but appetite invited whisky to mix with his art, and so upon dead walls he painted the trade-mark bull, and in front of museums he exaggerated the distortion of the human freak.

After the death of his mother, the boy was taken to the Foundlings' Home, where he was scolded by women and occasionally knocked down by a vagabond older than himself. Here he remembered to have seen his father but once. It was a Sunday when he came, years after the gentle creature, holding her child in her arms, had died at midnight. The painter laughed and cried and begged an old woman for a drink of brandy. He went away, and after an age had seemed to pass the matron of the place took the boy on her lap and told him that his father was dead, and then, putting him down, she added: "Run along, now, and be good."

The boy was taken by an old Italian woman. In after years he could not determine the length of time that he had lived in her wretched home, but with vivid brightness dwelled in his memory the morning when he ran away and found a free if not an easy life in the newsboys' lodging-house. He sold newspapers, he went to a night school, and as he grew older he picked up "river items" for an afternoon newspaper. His hope was that he might become a "professional journalist," as certain young men termed themselves; and study, which in an ill-lighted room, tuned to drowsiness by the buzzing of youthful mumblers, might have been a chafing task to one who felt not the rowel of a spurring ambition, was to him a pleasure full of thrilling promises. To him the reporter stood at the high-water mark of ambition's "freshet." But when years had passed and he had scrambled to that place he looked down and saw that his height was not a dizzy one. And instead of viewing a conquered province, he saw, falling from above, the shadows of trials yet to be endured. He worked faithfully, and at one time held the place of city editor, but a change in the management of the paper not only reduced him to the ranks, but, as the saying went, set him on the sidewalk. Then he wrote "specials." His work was bright, original and strong, and was reproduced throughout the country, but as it was not signed, the paper alone received the credit. Year after year he lived in this unsettled way— reading in the public library, musing at his own fireside, catching glimpses of an important work which the future seemed to hold, and waiting for the outlines of that work to become more distinct; but the months went by and the plan of the work remained in the shadow of the coming years.

DeGolyer had now reached that time of life when a wise man begins strongly to suspect that the past is but a future stripped of its delusions. He was a man of more than ordinary appearance; indeed, people who knew him, and who believed that size grants the same advantages to all

Opie Read

vocations, wondered why he was not more successful. He was tall and strong, and in his bearing there was an ease which, to one who recognizes not a sleeping nerve force, would have suggested the idea of laziness. His complexion was rather dark, his eyes were black, and his hair was a dark brown. He was not handsome, but his sad face was impressive, and his smile, a mere melancholy recognition that something had been said, did not soon fade from memory.

One afternoon DeGolyer called at the office of a morning newspaper, and was told that the managing editor wanted to see him. When he was shown in he found an aspiring politician laughing with forced heartiness at something which the editor had said. To the Southern politician the humor of an influential editor is full of a delirious mellowness.

When the politician went out the editor invited DeGolyer to take a seat. "Mr. DeGolyer, a number of your sketches have been well received."

"Yes, sir; they have made me a few encouraging enemies."

The editor smiled. "And you regard enemies as an encouragement, eh?"

"Yes, as a proof of success. Our friends mark out a course for us, and if we depart from it and do something better than their specifications call for, they become our enemies."

"I don't know but you are right." After a short silence the editor continued: "Mr. DeGolyer, we have been thinking of sending a man down into Costa Rica. Our merchants believe that if we were to pay more attention to that country we might thereby improve our trade. What we want is a number of letters intended to familiarize us with those people—want to show, you understand, that we are interested in them."

They talked during an hour. The nest day DeGolyer was on board a steamer bound for Punta Arenas. On the vessel he met a young man who said that his name was Henry Sawyer; and this young man was so blithe and light-hearted that DeGolyer, yielding to the persuasion of contrast, was drawn toward him. Young Sawyer was accompanied by his uncle, a short, fat, and at times a crusty old fellow. DeGolyer did not think that the uncle was wholly sound of mind. One evening, just before reaching port, and while the two young men were standing on deck, looking landward, young Sawyer said:

"Do you know, I think more of you than of any fellow I ever met?"

"I don't know it," DeGolyer answered, "but I am tempted to hope so."

"Good. I do, and that's a fact. You see, I've led a most peculiar sort of life. I never had any home—that is, any real home. I don't remember a thing about my father and mother. They died when I was very young, and then my uncle took me. Uncle never married and never was particularly attached to any one place. We have traveled a good deal; have lived quite a while in New Orleans, but for the past two years we have lived in a little bit of a place called Ulmata, in central Costa Rica. Uncle's got an interest in some mines not far from there. Say, why wouldn't it be a good idea for you to go to Ulmata and write your letters from there? Ain't any railroad, but there's a mule line running to the coast. How does it strike you?"

"I'd like to, but I'm afraid that it would take my letters too long to reach New Orleans; still, I don't know what difference that would make, as I'm not going to write news. After all," he added, as though he were arguing with himself, "I should think that the interior is more interesting than the coast, for people don't hang their characteristics over the coast line."

"There, you've hit the nail the very first lick. You go out there with us, and I'll bet we have a magnificent time."

"But your uncle might object."

"How can he? It ain't any of his business where you go."

"Of course not."

"Well, then, that settles it. But really, he'd like to have you. You'll like him; little peculiar at times, but you'll find him all right. You'll get a good deal of money for those letters, won't you?"

"No; a hired mail on a newspaper doesn't get much money."

"But it must take a good deal of brains to do your work."

"Presumably, but there stands a long row of brains ready to take the engagement—to take it, in fact, at a cut rate. The market is full of brains."

"How old did you say you were?"

"I am nearly thirty," DeGolyer answered.

"I'm only twenty-five, but that don't make any difference; we'll have a splendid time all the same. You read a good deal, I notice. Uncle's got a whole raft of books, and you can read to me when you get tired of reading to yourself. I've gone to school a good deal, but I'm not much of a hand with a book; but I tell you what I believe—I believe I could run a business to the queen's taste if I had a chance, and I'm going to try it one of these days. Uncle tells me that after awhile I may be worth some money, and if I am I'll get rich as sure as you're born. Business was born in me, but I've never had a chance to do anything, I have traded around a little, and I've made some money, too, but the trouble is that I've never been settled down long enough to do much of anything, I've scarcely any chance at all out at Ulmata. What would you rather be than anything else?"

"I don't know. It doesn't seem that nature has exerted herself in fitting me for anything, and I am a strong believer in natural fitness. We may learn to do a thing in an average sort of way, but excellence requires instinct, and instinct, of course, can't be learned."

"I guess that's so. I can see hundreds of ways to make money. I'd rather be a big merchant than anything else. Old fellow," he suddenly broke off, "I am as happy as can be to have you go out yonder with us; and mark what I tell you—we're going to have a splendid time."

CHAPTER II

A SLEEPY VILLAGE AND A FUSSY OLD MAN

In the village of Ulmata there was just enough of life to picture the dreamy indolence of man. Rest was its complexion, and freedom from all marks of care its most pleasing aspect.

Old Sawyer was so demonstrably gratified to have a companion for his nephew that he invited DeGolyer to take a room in his house, and DeGolyer gratefully accepted this kindness. Young Sawyer was delighted when the household had thus been arranged, and with many small confidences and unstudied graces of boyish friendship, he kept his guest in the refreshing atmosphere of welcome. And in the main the uncle was agreeable and courteous, but there were times when he flew out of his orbit of goodfellowship.

Once he came puffing into the room where DeGolyer was writing, and blusteringly flounced upon a sofa. He remained quiet for a few moments, and then he blew so strong a spout of annoyance that DeGolyer turned to him and asked:

"Has anything gone wrong?"

The old fellow's eyes bulged out as if he were straining under a heavy load. "Yes," he puffed, "the devil's gone wrong."

"But isn't that of ancient date?" DeGolyer asked.

"Here, now, young fellow, don't try to saw me!" And then he broke off with this execration: "Oh, this miserable world—this infernal pot where men are boiled!" He rolled his eyes like a choking ox, and after a short silence, asked: "Young fellow, do you know what I'd do if I were of your age?"

"If you were of my temperament as well as of my age I don't think you'd do much of anything."

"Yes, I would; I would confer a degree of high favor on myself. I would cut my throat, sir."

"Pardon me, but is it too late at your time of life?"

"Yes, for my nerve is diseased and I am a coward, an infamous, doddering old coward, sir. Good God! to live for years in darkness, bumping against the sharp corners of conscience. I have never told Henry, but I don't mind telling you that at times I am almost mad. For years I have sought to read myself out of it, but to an unsettled mind a book is a sly poison—the greatest of books are but the records of trouble. Don't you say a word to Henry. He thinks that my mind is as sound as a new acorn, but it isn't."

"I won't—but, by the way, he is young; why don't you advise him to kill himself?"

The old fellow flounced off the sofa and stood bulging his eyes at DeGolyer.

"Don't you ever say such a thing as that again!" he snorted. "Why, confound your hide! would you have that boy dead?"

DeGolyer threw down his pen. "No, I would have him live forever in his thoughtless and beautiful paradise; I would not pull him down to the thoughtful man's hell of self-communion."

"Look here, young man, you must have a history."

"No, simply an ill-written essay."

"Who was your father?"

"A fool."

"Ah, I grant you. And who was your mother?"

"An angel."

"No, sir, she—I beg your pardon," the old man quickly added. "You are sensitive, sir."

DeGolyer, sadly smiling, replied: "He who suffered in child-hood, and who in after life has walked hand in hand with disappointment, and is then not sensitive, is a brute."

"How well do I know the truth of that! DeGolyer, I have been acquainted with you but a short time, but you appeal to me strongly, sir. And I could almost tell you something, but it is something that I ought to keep to myself. I could make you despise me and then offer me your regard as a compromise. Oh, that American republic of ours, fought for by men who scorned the romance of kingly courts, is not so commonplace a country after all. Many strange things happen there, and some of them are desperately foul. Is that Henry coming? Hush."

The young man bounded into the room. "Say," he cried, "I've

bargained for six of the biggest monkeys you ever saw. That old fellow "—

"Henry," the uncle interrupted, taking up a hat and fanning his purplish face, "you are getting too old for that sort of foolishness. You are a man, you must remember, and it may not be long until you'll be called upon to exercise the judgment of a man."

"Oh, I was going to buy the monkeys and sell them again for three times as much as I gave for them, but you bet that when I'm called on to exercise the judgment, of a man I'll be there. And do you think that I'd fool with mines or anything else in this country? I wouldn't. I'd go to some American city and make money. Say, DeGolyer, when are you going to start off on that jaunt?"

"What jaunt?" the old man asked.

"I am going to make a tour of the country," DeGolyer answered. "I'm going to visit nearly every community of interest and gather material for my letters, and shall be gone a month or so, I should think."

"And I'm going with him," said Henry.

"No," the old man replied, "you are not going to leave me here all that time alone. I'm old, and I want you near me."

"All right, uncle; whatever you say goes."

When DeGolyer mounted a mule and set out on his journey, young Sawyer, as if clinging to his friendship, walked beside him for some distance into the country.

"Well, I'd better turn back here," said the young man,

halting. "Say, Hank, don't stay away any longer than you can help. It's devilish lonesome here, you know."

"I won't, my boy."

"All right. And say, if you can't do the thing up as well as you want to, throw up the job and come back here, for I'll turn loose, the first thing you know, and make enough money for both of us."

"God bless you, I hope that you may always make enough for yourself."

"And you bet I will, and for you, too. I hate like the mischief to see you go away. Couldn't think any more of you if we were twin brothers. And you think a good deal of me, too, don't you, Hank?"

"My boy," said DeGolyer, leaning over and placing his hand on the young fellow's shoulder, "I have never speculated with my friendship, and I don't know how valuable it is, but all of it that is worth having is yours. You make friends everywhere; I don't. You have nothing to conceal, and I have nothing to make known. To tell you the truth, you are the only real friend I ever had."

"Look out, now. That sort of talk knocks me; but say, don't be away any longer than you can help."

"I won't!" He rode a short distance, turned in his saddle, waved his hand and cried: "God bless you, my boy."

CHAPTER III

ALL WAS DARKNESS

Delays and difficulties of traveling, together with his own determination to do the work thoroughly, prolonged DeGolyer's absence. Nearly three months had passed. Evening was come, and from a distant hill-top the returning traveler saw the steeple of Ulmata's church—a black mark on the fading blush of lingering twilight. A chilly darkness crept out of the valley. Hungry dogs barked in the dreary village. DeGolyer could see but a single light. It burned in the priest's house—a dark age, and as of yore, with all the light held by the church. The weary man liberated his mule on a common, where its former companions were grazing, and sought the house of his friends. The house was dark and the doors were fastened. He knocked, and a startling echo, an audible darkness, came from the valley. He knocked again, and a voice cried from the street:

"Who's that?"

"Helloa, is that you, my boy?"

There was no answer, but a figure rushed through the darkness, seized DeGolyer, and in a hoarse whisper said:

"Come where there's a light."

"Why, what's the matter, Henry?"

"Come where there's a light."

DeGolyer followed him to a wretched place that bore the name of a public-house, and went with him into a room. A lamp sputtered on a shelf. Young Sawyer caught DeGolyer's hands.

"I have waited so long for you to come back to this dreadful place. I am all alone. Uncle is dead."

DeGolyer sat down without saying a word. He sat in silence, and then he asked:

"When did he die?"

"About two weeks after you left."

"Did he kill himself?"

"Good God, no! Why did you think that?"

"Oh, I didn't really think it—don't know why I said it."

"He was sick only a few days, and the strangest thing has come to light! He seemed to know before he was taken sick that he was going to die, and he spent nearly a whole day in writing—writing something for me—and the strangest thing has come to light. I can hardly realize it. Here it is; read it. Don't say a word till you have read every line of it. Strangest thing I ever heard of."

And this is what DeGolyer read by the light of the sputtering lamp:

"Years ago there lived in Salem, Mass., two brothers, George and Andrew Witherspoon. Their parents had passed away when the boys were quite young, but the youngsters had managed to get a fair start in life. Without ado let me say that I am Andrew Witherspoon. My brother and I were of different temperaments. He had graces of mind, but was essentially a business man. I prided myself that I was born to be a thinker. I worshiped Emerson. I know now that a man who would willingly become a thinker is a fool. When I was twenty-three—and George nearly twenty-one—I fell in love with Caroline Springer. There was just enough of poetry in my nature to throw me into a devotion that was almost wild in its intensity, and after my first meeting with her I knew no peace. The chill of fear and the fever of confidence came alternating day by day, and months passed ere I had the strength of nerve to declare myself; but at last the opportunity and the courage came together. I was accepted. She said that if I had great love her love might be measured by my own, and that if I did not think that I could love her always she would go away and end her days in grief. The wedding day was appointed. But when I went to claim my bride she was gone—gone with my brother George. To-day, an old man, I look back upon that time and see myself raving on the very brink of madness. I had known that George was acquainted with Caroline Springer—indeed, I had proudly introduced him to her. I will tell my story, though, and not discourse. But it is hard for an old man to be straightforward. If he has read much he is discursive, and if he has not read he is tedious with many words. I didn't leave Salem at once. I met George, and he did not even attempt to apologize for the wrong he had done me. He repeated the fool saying that all is fair in love. 'You ought to be glad that you discovered her lack of love in time,' he said. This was consolation, surely. My mind may never have been well-balanced, and I think that at this time it tilted over to one side, never to tilt back. And now my love, trampled in the mire, arose in the form of an evil determination. I would do my brother and his wife an injury that could not be repaired. I did not wish them dead; I wanted them to live and be miserable. A year passed, and a boy was born. I left my native town and went west. I lived there nearly three years, and then I sent to a Kansas newspaper an account of my death. It was printed, and I sent my brother a marked copy of the paper. Two weeks later I was in Salem. I wore a beard, kept myself close, and no one recognized me. I waited for an opportunity. It came, and I stole my brother's boy. I went to Boston, to Europe, back to America; lived here and there, and you know the rest. My dear boy, I repented somewhat, and it was my intention, at some time, to restore you to your parents, but you yourself were their enemy; you crept into my heart and I could not pluck you out. For a time the story of your mysterious disappearance filled the newspapers. You were found in a hundred towns, year after year, and when your sensation had run its course, you became the joke of the paragraphers. It was no longer, 'Who struck Billy Patterson?" but 'Who stole Henry Witherspoon?' Once I saw your father in New Orleans. He had come to identify his boy; but he went away with another consignment added to his large stock of disappointment. Finally all hope was apparently abandoned and even the newspapers ceased to find you.

"Your father and mother now live in Chicago. George Witherspoon is one of the great merchants of that city, and is more than a millionaire. This is why I have so often told you that one day you would be worth money. You were young and could afford to wait; I was old, and to me the present was everything, and you were the present.

"For some time I have been threatened with sudden death; I have felt it at night when you were asleep; and now I have written a confession which for years I irresolutely put aside from day to day. I charge you to bury me as Andrew

Witherspoon, for in the grave I hope to be myself, with nothing to hide. Write at once to your father, and after settling up my affairs, which I urge you not to neglect, you can go to him. In the commercial world a high place awaits you, and though I have done you a great wrong, I hope that your recollection of my deep love for you may soften your resentment and attune your young heart to the sweet melody of forgiveness.

"ANDREW WITHERSPOON."

DeGolyer folded the paper, returned it to Henry and sat in silence. He looked at the smoking lamp and listened to the barking of the hungry dogs.

"What do you think, Hank?"

"I don't know what to think."

"But ain't it the strangest thing you ever heard of?"

"Yes, it is strange, and yet not so strange to me. It is simply the sequel to a well-known story. In the streets of New Orleans, years ago, when I could scarcely carry a bundle of newspapers, I cried your name. The story was getting old then, for I remember that the people paid but little attention to it."

They sat for a time in silence. Young Witherspoon spoke, but DeGolyer did not answer him. They heard a guitar and a Spanish love song.

"Yes, it is strange," said DeGolyer, coming hack from a wandering reverie. "It is strange that I should be here with you;" and under a quickening of his newspaper instincts, he added, "and I shall have the writing of it."

"But wait awhile before you let your mind ran on on that, Hank. I don't want to be described and talked about so much. I know it can't be kept out of the papers, but we'll discuss that after a while. Now, let me tell you what I've done. I wrote to—to—father—don't that sound strange? I wrote to him and sent him a copy of uncle's paper—I would have sent the original, but I wanted to show that to you. I also sent a note that mother—there it is again—wrote to uncle a long time ago, and a lock of hair and some other little tricks. I told him to write to me, and here's his letter. It came nearly four weeks ago. And think, Hank, I've got a sister—grown and handsome, too, I'll bet."

Ecstasy had almost made the letter incoherent. It was written first by one and then another hand, with frequent interchanges; and DeGolyer; who fancied that he could pick character oat of the marks of a pen, thought that a mother's heart had overflowed and that a hard, commercial hand had cramped itself to a strange employment—the expression of affection. The father deplored the fact that his son could not be reached by telegraph, and still more did he lament his inability, on account of urgent business demands, to come himself instead of sending a letter. "Admit of no delay, but set out for home at once," the father commanded. "Telegraph as soon as you can, and your mother and I will meet you in New Orleans. I hope that this may not be exploited in the newspapers. God knows that in our time we have had enough of newspaper notoriety. Say nothing to any one, but come at once, and we can give for publication such a statement as we think necessary. Of course your discovery, as a sequel to your abduction years ago and the tremendous interest aroused at the time, will be of national importance, but I prefer that the news be sent out from this place."

Here the handwriting was changed, and "love," "thank God," "darling child," and emotion blots filled out the remainder of the page.

"You see," said Witherspoon, "that I have a reason for depriving you of an early whack at this thing. Now, I have written again and told them not to be impatient, and that I would leave here as soon as possible. I have settled up everything here, but I've got to go to a little place away over on the coast and close out some mining interests there."

"It must be of but trifling importance, my boy, and I should think that you'd let it go."

"No, sir; I'm going to do my duty by that dear old man if I never do anything else while I live."

He held not a mote of resentment. Indeed was his young heart "attuned to the sweet melody of forgiveness."

"By the way, Hank, here's a letter for you."

The communication was brief. It was from New Orleans and ran thus: "The five letters which we have published have awakened no interest whatever, and I am therefore instructed to discontinue the service. Inclosed please find check for the amount due you."

"What is it, Hank?"

"Oh, nothing except what I might have expected. Read it."

Witherspoon read the letter, and crumpling it, broke out in his impulsive way: "That's all right, old fellow. It fits right into my plan, and now let me tell you what that is. We'll leave here to-morrow and go over to Dura and settle up there. I don't know how long it will take, and I won't try to telegraph until we get through. Dura isn't known as a harbor, it is such a miserably small place, but ships land there once in awhile, and we can sail from there. But the main part of my plan is that you are to go with me and live in Chicago; and I'll bet we have a magnificent time. I'll go in the store, and I'll warrant that father—don't that sound strange?—that father can get you a good place on one of the newspapers. You haven't had a chance. Hank, and when you do get one, I'll bet you can lay out the best of them. What do you say?"

"Henry," said the dark-visaged DeGolyer—and the light of affection beamed in his eyes—"Henry, you are a positive charm; and if I should meet a girl adorned with a disposition like yours, I would unstring my heart, hand it to her and say, 'Here, miss, this belongs to you.'"

"Oh, you may find one. I've got a sister, you know. What! are you trying to look embarrassed? Do you know what I'm going to say? I'm going to lead you up to my sister and say, 'Here, I have caught you a prince; take him.'"

"Nonsense, my boy."

"That's all right; but, seriously, will you go with me?"

"I will."

"Good. We'll get ready to-night and start early in the morning. But I mustn't forget to see the priest again. He was a friend when I needed one; he took charge of uncle's burial. But," he suddenly broke off with rising spirits, "won't we have a time? Millionaire, eh? I'll learn that business and make it worth ten millions."

CHAPTER IV

A STRANGE REQUEST

The next morning, before it was well light, and at a time when brisk youth and slow age were seeking the place of confession, Henry Witherspoon went to the priest, not to acknowledge a sin, but to avow a deep gratitude. The journey was begun early; it was in July. The morning was braced with a cool breeze, the day was cloudless, and night's lingering gleam of silver melted in the gold of morn. Young Witherspoon's impressive nature was up with joy or down with sadness. The prospect of his new life was a happiness, and the necessity to leave his old uncle in a foreign country was a sore regret; so happiness and regret strove against each other, but happiness, advantaged with a buoyant heart as a contest-ground, soon ended the struggle.

On a brown hill-top they met the sunrise, and from a drowsy roosting-place they flushed a flock of greenish birds. Witherspoon stood in his stirrups and waved his hat. "Good-by," he cried, "but you needn't have got up so soon. We didn't want you. Hank," he said, turning sideways in his saddle, "I think we can get there in about five days, at the pace we'll be compelled to go; and we can sell these mules or give them away, just as we like. Going home! I can't get the strangeness of it out of my head. And a sister, too, mind you.

I'm beginning to feel like a man now. You see, uncle wanted me to be a boy as long as I could, and it was only of late that he began to tell me that I must put aside foolishness; but I am beginning to feel like a man now."

"You will need to feel like one when you take up your new responsibilities. You are playing now, but it may be serious enough after a while."

"What! Don't preach, Hank. Responsibilities! Why, I'll throw them over my shoulder like a twine string. But let me tell you something. There's one thing I'm not going to allow— they shan't say a word against that old man. Oh, I know the trouble and grief he brought about, but by gracious, he had a cause. If—if—mother didn't love him, why did she say that if he didn't love her she would go away somewhere and grieve herself to death? That was no way to treat a fellow, especially a fellow that loves you like the mischief. And besides, why did father cut him out? Pretty mean thing for a man to slip around and steal his brother's sweetheart. In this country it would mean blood."

"You are a jewel, my boy."

"No, I'm simply just. Of course, two wrongs don't make a right, as the saying has it, but a wrong with a cause is half-way right, and I'll tell them at the very start that they better not talk about the matter. In fact, I told them so in the letter. You've had a pretty hard time of it, haven't you, Hank?"

"I shouldn't want an enemy's dog to have a harder one," DeGolyer answered.

"But you've got a good education."

"So has the hog that picks up cards and tells the time of day," said DeGolyer, "but what good does that do him? He has to work harder than other hogs, and is kept hungry so that he may perform with more sprightliness. But if I have a good education, my boy, I stole it, and I shouldn't be surprised at any time to meet an officer with a warrant of arrest sworn out against me by society."

"Good; but you didn't steal trash at any rate. But, Hank, you look for the dark when the light would serve you better. Don't do it. Throw off your trouble."

"Oh, I'm not disposed to look so much for the dark as you may imagine. Throw it off! That's good advice. It is true that we may sometimes throw off a trouble, but we can't very well throw off a cause. Some natures are like a piece of fly-paper—a sorrow alights and sticks there. But that isn't my nature. It doesn't take much to make me contented."

The weather remained pleasant, and the travelers were within a day's ride of Dura, when Witherspoon complained one morning of feeling ill, and by noon be could scarcely sit in his saddle.

"Let us stop somewhere," DeGolyer urged.

"No," Witherspoon answered, "let us get to Dura as soon as we can. I've got a fever, haven't I?"

DeGolyer leaned over and placed his hand on Witherspoon's forehead. "Yes, you have."

"The truth is, I haven't felt altogether right since the first day after we started, but I thought it would wear off."

When they reached Dura, Witherspoon was delirious. Not a ship was in port, and DeGolyer took him to an inn and summoned such medical aid as the hamlet afforded. The physician naturally gave the case a threatening color, and it followed that he was right, for at the close of the fourth day the patient gave no promise of improvement. The innkeeper said that sometimes a month passed between the landing of ships at that point. The fifth day came. DeGolyer sat by the bedside of his friend, fanning him. The doctor had called and had just taken his leave.

"Give me some water, Hank."

"Ah, you are coming around all right, my boy," DeGolyer cried. He brought the water; and when the patient drank and shook his head as a signal to take away the cup, DeGolyer asked; "Don't you feel a good deal better?"

"No."

"But your mind is clear?"

"Yes."

"Shall I put another cold cloth on your head?"

"If you please."

And when DeGolyer had gently done this, Witherspoon said: "Sit down here, Hank."

"All right, my boy, here I am."

"Hank, I'm not going to get well."

"Oh, yes, you are, and don't you let any such nonsense enter your head."

"It's a good ways from nonsense, I tell you. I know what I'm talking about; I know just as well as can be that I'm going to die—now you wait till I get through. It can't be helped, and there's no use in taking on over it. I did want to see my father and mother and sister, but it can't be helped."

DeGolyer was on his knees beside the bed. He attempted to speak, but his utterance was choked; and the tears in his eyes blurred to spectral dimness the only human being whom he held warm in his heart.

"Hank, while I am able to talk I've got a great favor to ask of you. And you'll grant it, won't you?"

"Yes," DeGolyer Bobbed.

For a few moments the sick man lay in silence. He fumbled about and found DeGolyer's hand. "My father and mother are waiting for me," he said. "They have been raised into a new life. If I never come it will be worse than if I had never been found, for they'll have a new grief to bear, and it may be heavier than the first. They must have a son, Hank."

"My dear boy, what do you mean?"

"I mean that if I die—and I know that I am going to die—you must be their son. You must go there, not as Henry DeGolyer, but as Henry Witherspoon, their own son."

"Merciful God! I can't do that."

"But if you care for me you will. Take all my papers—take everything I've got—and go home. It will be the greatest favor you could do me and the greatest you could do them."

"But, my dear boy, I should be a liar and a hypocrite."

"No, you would be playing my part because I couldn't play it. Once you said that you would give me your life if I wanted it, and now I want it. You can make them happy, and they'll be so proud of you. Won't you try it? I would do anything on earth for you, and now you deny me this—and who knows but my spirit might enter into you and form a part of your own? How can you refuse me when you know that I think more of you than I do of anybody? This is no boy's prank—I'm a man now. Will you?"

"Henry," said DeGolyer, "this is merely a feverish notion that has come out of your derangement. Put it by, and after a while we will laugh at it. Is the cloth hot again?"

"Yes."

"I'll change it." And DeGolyer, removing the cloth and placing his hand on his friend's forehead, added: "Your fever isn't so high as it was yesterday. You are coming out all right."

"No, I tell you that I'm going to die; and you won't do me the only favor I could ask. Don't you remember saying, not long ago, that a man's life is a pretense almost from the beginning to the end?"

"I don't remember saying it, but it agrees with what I have often been compelled to think."

"Well, then, if you think that life is a pretense, why not pretend by request?"

"Well talk about it some other time, my boy."

"But there may not be any other time."

"Oh, yes, there will be. Don't you think you can sleep now?"

"No, I don't think I can sleep and wake up again."

But he did sleep, and he did awake again. Three more days passed wearily away, and the patient was delirious most of the time. DeGolyer's acquaintance with Spanish was but small, and he could comprehend but little of what a pedantic doctor might say, yet he learned that there was not much encouragement to be drawn from the fact that the sick man's mind sometimes returned from its troubled wandering.

DeGolyer was again alone with his friend. It was a hot though a blustery afternoon, and the sea, in sight through the open door, sounded the deeper notes of its endless opera.

"Hank."

"I'm here, my boy."

"Have you thought about what I told you to do?"

"Are you still clinging to that notion?"

"No; it is clinging to me. Have you thought about it?"

"Yes."

"And what did you think?"

"I thought that for you I would take the risk of playing a part that you are unable to perform. But really, Henry, I'm too old."

"You have promised, and my mind is at ease," the sick man said, with a smile. "Now I feel that I have given my life over to you and that I shall not really be dead so long as you are alive. Among my things you will find some letters written by my mother to my uncle, and a small gold chain and a locket that I wore when I was sto—when uncle took me. That's all."

"I will do the best I can, but I'm too old."

"You are only a few years older than I am. They'll never know. They'll be blind. You'll have the proof. Go at once. You are Henry Witherspoon. That's all."

The blustery afternoon settled into a calm as the sun went down, and a change came with the night. The sufferer's mind flitted back for a moment, and in that speck of time he spoke not, but he gave his friend a look of gratitude. All was over. During the night DeGolyer sat alone by the bedside. And a ship came at morning.

A kind-hearted priest offered his services. "The ship has merely dodged in here," said he, "and won't stay long, and it may be a month before another one comes." And then he added: "You may leave these melancholy rites to me."

A man stepped into the doorway and cried in Spanish: "The ship is ready."

DeGolyer turned to the priest, and placing a purse on the table, said: "I thank you." Then he stepped lightly to the bedside and gazed with reverence and affection upon the face of the dead boy. He spoke the name of Christ, and the priest heard him say: "Take his spirit to Thy love and Thy mercy, for no soul more forgiving has ever entered Thy Father's kingdom." He took up his traveling-bag and turned toward the door. "One moment," said the priest, and pointing to the couch, he asked: "What name?"

"Henry—Henry DeGolyer."

CHAPTER V

DISSECTING A MOTIVE

Onward went the ship, nodding to the beck and call of mighty ocean. DeGolyer—or, rather, Henry Witherspoon, as now he knew himself—walked up and down the deck. And it seemed that at every turn his searching grief had found a new abiding-place for sorrow. His first strong attachment was broken, and he felt that in the years to come, no matter what fortune they might bring him, there could not grow a friendship large enough to fill the place made vacant by his present loss. An absorbing love might come, but love is by turns a sweet and anxious selfishness, while friendship is a broad-spread generosity. Suddenly he was struck by the serious meaning of his obligation, and with stern vivisection he laid bare the very nerves of his motive. At first he could find nothing save the discharge of a sacred duty; but what if this trust had entailed a life of toil and sacrifice? Would he have accepted it? In his agreement to this odd compact was there not an atom of self-interest? Over and over again he asked himself these questions, and he strove to answer them to the honor of his incentive, but he felt that in this strife there lay a prejudice, a hope that self might be cleared of all dishonor. But was there ever a man who, in the very finest detail, lived a life of perfect truth and freedom from all selfishness? If so, why should Providence have put him in a

Opie Read

grasping world? Give conscience time and it will find an easy bed, and yet the softest bed may have grown hard ere morning comes.

"Who am I that I should carp with myself?" the traveler mused. "Have the world and its litter of pups done anything for me?" He walked up and down the deck. "God knows that I shall always love the memory of that dear boy. But if all things are foreseen and are still for the best, why should he have died? Was it to throw upon me this great opportunity? But who am I? And why should a special opportunity be wrought for me? But who is anybody?"

Going whither? Home. A father—and he thought of a drunken painter. A mother—and his mind flew back to a midnight when arms that had carried him warm with life were cold in death. A millionaire's son—that thought startled him. What were the peculiar duties of a millionaire's son? No matter. They might impose a strain, but they could never be so trying as constant poverty. But who had afflicted him with poverty? First his birth and then his temperament. But who gave him the temperament? He wheeled about and walked away as if he would be rid of an impertinent questioner.

When the ship reached New Orleans he went straightway to the telegraph office and sent this message to George Witherspoon: "Will leave for Chicago to-day."

And now his step was beyond recall; he must go forward. But conscience had no needles, and his mind was at rest. In expectancy there was a keen fascination. He met a reporter whom he knew, but there was no sign of recognition. A beard, thick, black and neatly trimmed, gave Henry's face an unfamiliar mold. But he felt a momentary fear, he realized that a possible danger thenceforth would lie in wait for him, and then came the easing assurance that his early life, his father and his mother, were remembered by no one of importance, and that even if he were recognized as Henry DeGolyer, he could still declare himself the stolen son of George Witherspoon. Indeed, with safety he could thus announce himself to the managing editor who had sent him to Costa Rica, and he thought of doing this, but no, his—his father wanted the secret kept until the time was ripe for its divulgence. He went into a restaurant, and for the first time in his life he felt himself free to order regardless of the prices on the bill of fare. Often, when a hungry boy, he had sold newspapers in that house, and enviously he had watched the man who seemed to care not for expenses. As he sat there waiting for his meal, a newsboy came in, and after selling him a paper, stood near the table.

"Sit down, little fellow, and have something to eat."

This was sarcasm, and the boy leered at him.

"Sit down, won't you?"

"What are you givin' me?"

"This," said Henry, and he handed him a dollar.

CHAPTER VI

WAITING AT THE STATION

Men bustling their way to the lunch counter; old women fidgeting in the fear that they had forgotten something; man in blue crying the destination of outgoing trains; weary mothers striving to soothe their fretful children; the tumult raised by cabmen that were crowding against the border-line of privilege; bells, shrieks, new harshnesses here and there; confusion everywhere—a railway station in Chicago.

"The train ought to be here now," said George Witherspoon, looking at his watch.

"Do you know exactly what train he is coming on?" his wife asked.

"Yes; he telegraphed again from Memphis."

"You didn't tell me you'd got another telegram."

"My dear, I thought I did. The truth is that I've been so rushed and stirred up for the last day or so that I've hardly known what I was about."

"And I can scarcely realize now what I'm waiting for," said a young woman. "Mother, you look as if you haven't slept any for a week."

"And I don't feel as if I have."

George Witherspoon, holder of the decisive note in the affairs of that great department store known as "The Colossus," may not by design have carried an air that would indicate the man to whom small tradesman regarded it as a mark of good breeding to cringe, but even in a place where his name was not known his appearance would strongly have appealed to commercial confidence. That instinct which in earlier life had prompted fearless speculation, now crystalized into conscious force, gave unconscious authority to his countenance. He was tall and with so apparent a strength in his shoulders as to suggest the thought that with them he had shoved his way to success. He was erect and walked with a firm step; he wore a heavy grayish mustache that turned under; his chin had a forceful squareness; he was thin-haired, nearing baldness. In his manner was a sort of firm affability, and his voice was of that tone which success nearly always assumes, kindly, but with a suggestion of impatience. His eyes were restless, as though accustomed to keep watch over many things. When spoken to it was his habit to turn quickly, and if occasion so warranted, to listen with that pleasing though frosty smile which to the initiated means, "I shall be terribly bored by any request that you may make, and shall therefore be compelled to refuse it." He was sometimes liberal, though rarely generous. If he showed that a large disaster touched his heart, he could not conceal the fact that a lesser mishap simply fell upon his irritated nerves; and therefore he might contribute to a stricken city while refusing to listen to the distress of a family.

Mrs. Witherspoon was a dark-eyed little woman. In her earlier life she must have been handsome, for in the expression of her face there was a reminiscence of beauty. Her dimples had turned traitor to youth and gossiped of coming age. Women are the first to show the contempt with which wealth regards poverty, the first to turn with resentment upon former friends who have been left in the race for riches, the first to feel the overbearing spirit that money stirs; but this woman had not lost her gentleness.

The girl was about nineteen years of age. She was a picture of style, delsarted to ease of motion. She was good-looking and had the whims and the facial tricks that are put to rhyme and raved over in a sweetheart, but which are afterward deplored in a wife.

"I feel that I shan't know how to act."

Witherspoon looked at his daughter and said, "Ellen."

"But, papa, I just know I shan't. How should I know? I never met a brother before; never even thought of such a thing."

"Don't be foolish. We are not the only people that have been placed in such a position. No matter how you may be situated, remember that you are not a pioneer; no human strain is new."

"But it's the only time *I* was ever placed in such a position."

"Nonsense. In this life we must learn to expect anything." Mrs. Witherspoon was silently weeping. "Caroline, don't, please. Remember that we are not alone. A trial of joy, my dear, is the easiest trial to bear."

"Not always," she replied.

A counter commotion in the general tumult—the train.

A crowd waited outside the iron gate. A tall young man came through with the hastening throng. He caught Witherspoon's wandering eye. Strangers looking for each other are guided by a peculiar instinct, but Witherspoon stood questioning that instinct. The mother could see nothing with distinctness. The young man held up a gold chain.

It was soon over. People who were hastening toward a train turned to look upon a flurry of emotion—a mother faint with joy; a strong man stammering words of welcome; a girl seemingly thrilled with a new prerogative; a stranger in a nest of affection.

"Come, let us get into the carriage," said Witherspoon. "Come, Caroline, you have behaved nobly, and don't spoil it all now."

She gave her husband a quick though a meek glance and took Henry's arm. When the others had seated themselves in the carriage, Witherspoon stood for a moment on the curbstone.

"Drive to the Colossus," he commanded. Mrs. Witherspoon put out her hand with a pleading gesture. "You are not going there before you go home, are you, dear?" she asked.

"I am compelled to go there, but I'll stay only a moment or two," he answered. "I'll simply hop out for a minute and leave the rest of you in the carriage. There's something on hand that needs my attention at once. Drive to the Colossus," he said as he stepped into the carriage. A moment later he remarked: "Henry, you are different from what I expected. I thought you were light."

"He is just like my mother's people," Mrs. Witherspoon spoke up. "All the Craigs were dark."

They drove on in a silence not wholly free from embarrassment. Through the carriage windows Henry caught glimpses of a world of hurry. The streets, dark and dangerous with traffic, stretched far away and ended in a cloud of smoke. "It will take time to realize all this," the young men mused, and meeting the upturned eyes of Mrs. Witherspoon, who had clasped her hands over his shoulder, he said:

"Mother, I hope you are not disappointed in me."

"You are just like the Craigs," she insisted. "They were dark. And Uncle Louis was so dark that he might have been taken for an Italian, and Uncle Harvey"—She hesitated and glanced at her husband.

"What were you going to say about your Uncle Harvey?" Henry asked.

"Nothing, only he was dark just like all the Craigs."

There is a grunt which man borrowed from the goat, or which, indeed, the goat may have borrowed from man. And this grunt, more than could possibly be conveyed by syllabic utterance, expresses impatience. Witherspoon gave this goat-like grunt, and Henry knew that he had heard of the Craigs until he was sick of their dark complexion. He knew, also, that the great merchant had not a defensive sense of humor, for humor, in the exercise of its kindly though effective functions, would long ago have put these Craigs to an unoffending death.

"I don't see why you turn aside to talk of complexion when the whole situation is so odd," said Ellen, speaking to her father. "I am not able to bring myself down to a realization of it yet, although I have been trying to ever since we got that letter from that good-for-nothing country, away off yonder. You must know that it strikes me differently from what it does any one else. It is all romance with me—pure romance."

Witherspoon said nothing, but his wife replied: "It isn't romance with me; it is an answer to a prayer that my heart has been beating year after year."

"But don't cry, mother," said Ellen. "Your prayer has been answered."

"Yes, I know that, but look at the long, long years of separation, and now he comes back to me a stranger."

"But we shall soon be well acquainted," Henry replied, "and after a while you may forget the long years of separation."

"I hope so, my son, or at least I hope to be able to remember them without sorrow. But didn't you, at times, fancy that you remembered me? Couldn't you recall my voice?" Her lips trembled.

"No," he answered, slowly shaking his head. This was the cause for more tears. She had passed completely out of his life. Ah, the tender, the hallowed egotism of a mother's love!

The carriage drew up to the sidewalk, and the driver threw open the door. "I'll be back in just a minute," said Witherspoon, as he got out; and when he was gone his wife began to apologize for him. "He's always so busy. I used to think that the time might come when he could have more leisure, but it hasn't."

"What an immense place!" said Henry, looking out.

"One of the very largest in the world," Ellen replied. "And the loveliest silks and laces you ever saw." A few moments later she said: "Here comes father."

"Drive out Michigan," Witherspoon commanded. They were whirled away and had not gone far when the merchant, directing Henry's attention, said:

"The Auditorium."

"The what?"

"The Auditorium. Is it possible you never heard of it?"

"Oh, yes, I remember now. It was formally opened by the President."

He did remember it; he remembered having edited telegraph for a newspaper on the night when Patti's voice was first heard in this great home of music.

"Biggest theater in the world," said Witherspoon.

"Bigger than La Scala of Milan?" Henry asked.

"Beats anything in the world, and I remember when the ground could have been bought for—see that lot over there?" he broke off, pointing. "I bought that once for eighty dollars a foot and sold it for a hundred."

"Pretty good sale! wasn't it?" Henry innocently asked.

"Good sale! What do you suppose it's worth now!"

"I have no idea."

"Three thousand a foot if it's worth a penny. There never was anything like it since the world began. I'm not what you might call an old-timer, but I've seen some wonderful changes here. Now, this land right here—fifteen hundred a foot; could have bought it not so very long ago for fifty. I tell you the world never saw anything like it. Why, just think of it; there are men now living who could have bought the best corner in this city for a mere song. There's no other town like this. Look at the buildings. When a man has lived here a while he can't live in any other town—any other town is too slow for him—and yet I heard an old man say that he could have got all the land he wanted here for a yoke of oxen."

"But he hadn't the oxen, eh?"

"Of coarse he had," Witherspoon replied, "but who wanted to exchange useful oxen for a useless mud-hole? Beats any-thing in this world."

Henry looked at him in astonishment. His tongue, which at first had seemed to be so tight with silence, was now so loose with talk. He had dropped no hint of his own importance; he had made not the slightest allusion to the energy and ability that had been required to build his mammoth institution. His impressive dignity was set aside; he was blowing his town's horn.

The carriage turned into Prairie Avenue. "Look at all this," Witherspoon continued, waving his hand. "I remember when it didn't deserve the name of a street. Look at that row of houses. Built by a man that used to drive a team. There's a beauty going up. Did you ever see anything like it?"

"I can well say that I never have," Henry answered.

"I should think not," said Witherspoon, and pointing to the magnificent home of some obscure man, he added: "I remember when an old shed stood there. Just look at that

Opie Read

carving in front."

"Who lives there?" Henry asked.

"Did hear, but have forgotten. Yonder's one of green stone. I don't like that so well. Here we have a sort of old stone. That house looks as though it might be a hundred years old, but it was put up last year. Well, here's our house."

The carriage drew up under the porte-cocher of a mansion built of cobble-stones. It was as strong as a battlement, but its outlines curved in obedience to gracefulness and yielded to the demand of striking effect. Viewed from one point it might have been taken for a castle; from another, it suggested itself as a spireless church. Strangers halted to gaze at it; street laborers looked at it in admiration. It was showy in a neighborhood of mansions.

Mrs. Witherspoon led Henry to the threshold and tremulously kissed him. And it was with this degree of welcome that the wanderer was shown into his home.

CHAPTER VII

A MOTHER'S AFFECTION

In one bedazzled moment we review a whole night of darkness. A luxury brings with it the memory of a privation. The first glimpse of those drawing-rooms, gleaming with white and warm with gold, were seen against a black cloud, and that cloud was the past. The wanderer was startled; there was nothing now to turn aside the full shock of his responsibilities. He felt the enormity of his pretense, and he began again to pick at his motive. Mrs. Witherspoon perceived a change in him and anxiously asked if he were ill. No, but now that his long journey was ended he felt worn by it. The father saw him with a fresh criticism and said that he looked older than his years bespoke him; but the mother, quick in every defense, insisted that he had gone through enough to make any one look old; and besides, the Craigs, being a thoughtful people, always looked older than they really were. In the years that followed, this first day "at home" was reviewed in all its memories—the library with its busts of old thinkers and its bright array of new books; the sober breakfast-room in which luncheon was served; the orderly servants; the plants; the gold fishes; the heavy hangings; a tiger skin with a life-expressive head; the portraits of American statesmen; the rich painting of a cow that flashed back the tradition of a trade-mark bull on a dead wall.

Evening came with melody in the music-room; midnight, and Henry sat alone in his room. He was heavy with sadness. The feeling that henceforth his success must depend upon the skill of his hypocrisy, and that he must at last die a liar, lay upon him with cold oppression. Kindness was a reproach and love was a censure. Some one tapped at the door.

"Come in."

Mrs. Witherspoon entered. "I just wanted to see if you were comfortable," she said, seating herself in a rocking-chair.

"So much so that I am tempted to rebel against it," he answered.

She smiled sadly. "There are so many things that I wanted to say to you, dear, but I haven't had a chance, somehow."

Her eyes were tear-stricken and her voice trembled. "It isn't possible that you could know what a mother's love is, my son."

"I *didn't* know, but you have taught me."

"No, not yet; but I will—if you'll let me."

"If I'll let you?" He looked at her in surprise.

"Yes, if you will bear with me. Sit here," she said, tapping the broad arm of the chair. He obeyed, and she took his arms and put them about her neck. "There hasn't been much love in my life, precious. Perhaps I am not showy enough, not strong enough for the place I occupy."

"But you are good enough to hold the place of an angel."

She attempted to speak, but failed. Something fell on her hand, and she looked up. The man was weeping. They sat there in silence.

"In your early life," she said, pressing his arms closer about her neck, "my love sought to protect you, but now it must turn to you for support. Your uncle—but you told me not to speak of him." She paused a moment, and then continued: "Your uncle did me a deep wrong, but I had wronged him. Oh, I don't know why I did. And he had kept my letters all these years." Another silence. She was the first to speak. "Ellen loves me, but a daughter's love is more of a help than a support."

"And father?"

"Oh, he is good and kind," she quickly answered, "but somehow I haven't kept up with him. He is so strong, and I fear that my nature is too simple; I haven't force enough to help him when he's worried. He hasn't said so, but I know it! And of course you don't understand me yet; but won't you bear with me?"

In her voice there was a sad pleading for love, and this man, though playing a part, dropped the promptings of his role, and with the memory of his own mother strong within him, pressed this frail woman to his bosom and with tender reverence kissed her.

"Oh," she sobbed, "I thank God for bringing you back to me. Good night."

He closed the door when she was gone, and stood as though he knew not whither to turn. He looked at the onyx clock ticking on the mantelpiece. He listened to the rumble of a carriage in the street. He put out his hands, and going slowly into his sleeping-room, sank upon his knees at the bedside.

Opie Read

CHAPTER VIII

THE DOMAIN OF A GREAT MERCHANT

To one who has gazed for many hours upon whirling scenes, and who at his journey's end has gone to sleep in an unfamiliar place, the question of self-identity presents itself at morning and of the dozing faculties demands an answer. Henry lay in bed, catching at flitting consciousness, but missing it. He tried to recall his own name, but could not. One moment he felt that he was on board a ship, rising and sinking with the mood of the sea; then he was on a railway train, catching sight of a fence that streaked its way across a field. He saw a boy struggling with a horse that was frightened at the train; he saw a girl wave her beflowered hat—a rushing woods, a whirling open space, a sleepy station. Once he fancied that he was a child lying in bed, not at midnight, but at happy, bird-chattered morning, when the sun was bright; but then he heard a roar and he saw a street stretch out into a darkening distance, and he knew that he was in a great city. Consciousness loitered within reach, and he seized it. He was called to breakfast.

How bright the morning. Through the high and church-like windows softened sunbeams fell upon the stairway. He heard Ellen singing in the music-room; he met the rich fragrance of coffee. Mrs. Witherspoon, with a smile of quiet happiness, stood at the foot of the stairs. Ellen came out with a lithe skip and threw a kiss at him. Witherspoon sat in the breakfast-room reading a morning newspaper.

"Well, my son, how do you find yourself this morning?" the merchant asked, throwing aside the newspaper and stretching himself back in his chair.

"First-rate; but I had quite a time placing myself before I was fully awake."

"I guess that's true of nearly everybody who comes to Chicago. It makes no difference how wide-awake a man thinks he is, he will find when he comes to this city that he has been nodding."

Breakfast was announced. Ellen took Henry's hand and said: "Come, this is your place here by me. Mother told me to sit near you; she wants me to check any threatened outbreak of your foreign peculiarities."

"Ellen, what do you mean? I didn't say anything of the sort, Henry. It could make no difference where my mother's people were brought up. The Craigs always knew how to conduct themselves."

"Oh, yes," Witherspoon spoke up, "the Craigs were undoubtedly all right, but we are dealing with live issues now. Henry, we'll go down to the store this morning"—

"So soon?" his wife interrupted.

"So soon?" the merchant repeated. "What do you mean by so soon? Won't it be time to go?"

"Oh, yes, I suppose so."

"And where do I come in?" asked the girl.

"You can go if you insist," said Witherspoon, "but there are matters that he and I must arrange at once. We've got to fix up some sort of statement for the newspapers; can't keep this thing a secret, you know, and a tailor must be consulted. Your clothes are all right, my son," he quickly added, "but—well, you understand."

Henry understood, but he had thought when he left New Orleans that he was well dressed. And now for a moment he felt ragged.

"When shall we have the reception?" Ellen asked.

"The reception," Henry repeated, looking up in alarm.

"Why, listen to him," the girl cried. "Don't you know that we must give a reception? Why, we couldn't get along without it; society would cut us dead. Think how nice it will be—invitations with 'To meet Mr. Henry Witherspoon' on them."

"Must I go through that?" Henry asked, appealing to Mrs. Witherspoon.

"Of course you must, but not until the proper time."

"Why, it will be just splendid," the girl declared. "You ought to have seen me the night society smiled and said, 'Well, we will now permit you to be one of us.' Oh, the idea of not showing you off, now that we've caught you, is ridiculous. You needn't appeal to mother. You couldn't keep her from parading you up and down in the presence of her friends."

He was looking at Mrs. Witherspoon. She smiled with more of humor than he had seen her face express, and thus delivered her opinion: "If we had no reception, people would think that we were ashamed of our son."

"All right, mother; if you want your friends to meet the wild man of Borneo who has just come to town, I have nothing more to say. Your word shall be a law with me; but I must tell you that whenever you make arrangements into which I enter, you must remember that society and I have had scarcely a hat-tipping acquaintance. I may know many things that society never even dreamed of, but some of society's simplest phases are dangerous mysteries to me."

"Nonsense," said Witherspoon. "Society may rule a poor man, but a rich man rules society. Common sense always commands respect, for nearly every rule that governs the conduct of man is founded upon it. Don't you worry about the reception or anything else. You are a man of the world, and to such a man society is a mere plaything."

"Well," replied Ellen, wrinkling her handsome brow with a frown, "I must say that you preach an odd sort of sermon. Society is supposed to hold the culture and the breeding of a community, sir."

"Yes, supposed to," Witherspoon agreed.

"Oh, well, if you question it I won't argue with you." And giving Henry a meaning look, she continued: "Of course business is first. Art drops on its worn knees and prays to business, and literature begs it for a mere nod. Everything is the servant of business."

"Everything in Chicago is," the merchant replied.

"Art is the old age of trade," said Henry. "A vigorous nation buys and sells and fights; but a nation that is threatened with decay paints and begs."

"Good!" Witherspoon exclaimed. "I think you've hit it squarely. Since we went to Europe, Ellen has had an idea that trade is rather low in the scale of human interest."

"Now, father, I haven't any such idea, and you know it, too. But I do think that people who spend their lives in getting money can't be as refined as those who have a higher aim."

Witherspoon grunted. "What do you call a higher aim? Hanging about a picture gallery and simpering over a lot of long-haired fellows in outlandish dress, ha? Is it refinement to worship a picture simply because you are not able to buy it? Some people rave over art, and we buy it and hang it up at home."

She laughed, and slipping off her chair, ran round to her father and put her arms about his neck. "I can always stir you up, can't I?"

"You can when you talk that way," he answered.

"But you know I don't mean that you aren't refined. Who could be more gentle than you are? But you must let me enjoy an occasional mischief. My mother's people, the Craigs, were all full of mischief, and"

"Ellen," said her mother.

Witherspoon laughed, and reaching back, pretended to pull the girl's ears. "Am I going down town with you?" she asked.

"No, not this morning. I'm going to drive Henry down in the light buggy. My boy, I've got as fine a span of bay horses as you ever saw. Cost me five thousand apiece. That's art for you; eh, Ellen?"

"They are beautiful," she admitted.

"Yes, and strung up with pride. Get ready, Henry, and we'll go."

When Witherspoon gathered up the lines and with the whip touched one of the horses, both jumped as though startled by the same impulse.

"There's grace for you," said Witherspoon. "Look how they plant their fore feet."

Henry did not answer. He was looking back at a palace, his home; and he, too, was touched with a whip—the thrilling whip of pride. It lasted but a moment. His memory threw up a home for the friendless, and upon a background of hunger, squalor and wretchedness his fancy flashed the picture of an Italian hag, crooning and toothless.

"We'll turn into Michigan here," said the merchant. "Isn't this a great thoroughfare? Yonder is where we lived before we built our new house. Just think what this will be when these elms are old." They sped along the smooth drive. "Ho, boys! Business is creeping out this way, and that is the reason I got over on Prairie. See, that man has turned his residence into a sort of store. A little farther along you will see fashionable humbuggery of all sorts. These are women fakes along here. Ho, boys, ho! There's where old man Colton lives. We'll meet him at the store. In the Colossus Company he is next to me. Smart old fellow, but he worked many years in the hammer-and-tongs way, and he probably never would have done much if he hadn't been shoved. Ho, boys, *ho*! People ought to be arrested for piling brick in the street this way. Colton was always afraid of venturing; shuddered at the thought of risking his money; wanted it where he could lay his hands on it at any time. Brooks, his son-in-law, is a sort of general manager over our entire establishment, and he is one of the most active and useful men I ever saw—bright, quick, characteristically American. I think you'll like him. That place over there"—cutting his whip toward an old frame house scalloped and corniced in fantastic flimsiness— "was sold the other day at about thirty per cent more than it would have brought a few years ago."

They turned into another street and were taken up, it seemed, by the swift trade currents that swirl at morning, rush through the noon, glide past the evening and rest for a time in the semi-calm of midnight. Chicago has begun to set the pace of a nervous nation's progress. It is a city whose growth has proved a fatal example to many an overweaning town. Materialistic, it holds no theory that points not to great results; adventurous, it has small patience with methods that slowness alone has stamped as legitimate. Worshiping a deification of real estate, and with a rude aristocracy building upon the blood of the sow and the tallow of the bull, its atmosphere discourages one artist while inviting another to rake up the showered rewards of a "boom" patronage. Feeling that naught but sleepiness and sloth should be censured, it resents even a kindly criticism. Quick to recognize the feasibility of a scheme; giving money, but holding time as a sacred inheritance. It is a re-gathering of the forces that peopled America and then made her great among nations; a mighty community with a growing literary force and with its culture and its real love for the beautiful largely confined to the poor in purse; grand in a thousand respects; with its history glaring upon the black sky of night; with the finest boulevards in America and the filthiest alleys—a giant in need of a bath.

The Colossus stood as a towering island with "a tide in the

affairs of men" sweeping past. And it seemed to Henry that the buggy was cast ashore as a piece of driftwood that touches land and finds a lodgment. At an earlier day, and not so long ago either, the flaw of unconscious irony might have been picked in the name Colossus, but now the establishment, covering almost a block and rising story upon story, filled in the outlines of its pretentious christening.

"Tap, tap, tap—cash, 46; tap, tap—cash, 63," was the leading strain in this din of extensive barter and petty transaction. The Colossus boasted that it could meet every commercial demand; supply a sewing-machine needle or set up a saw-mill; receipt for gas bills and water rates or fit out a general store. Under one roof it held the resources of a city. Henry was startled by its immensity, and as he followed Witherspoon through labyrinths of bright gauzes and avenues of somber goods, he perceived that a change in the tone of the hum announced the approach of the master. And it appeared that, no matter what a girl might be doing, she began hurriedly to do something else the moment she spied Witherspoon coming toward her. The quick signs of flirtation, signals along the downward track of morality, subsided whenever this ruler came within sight; and the smirk bargain-counter miss would actually turn from the grinning idiocy of the bullet-headed fellow who had come in to admire her and would deign to wait on a poorly dressed woman who had failed to attract her attention.

The offices of the management were on the first floor, and Henry was conducted thither and shown into Witherspoon's private apartment—into the calico, bombazine, hardware and universal nick-nack holy of holies. The room was not fitted up for show, but for business. Its furniture consisted mainly of a roll-top desk, a stamp with its handle sticking up like the tail of an excited cat, a dingy carpet and several chairs of a shape so ungenial to the human form as to suggest that a hint at me desirability of a visitor's early withdrawal might have been incorporated in their construction.

"I will see if Colton has come down," Witherspoon remarked, glancing through a door into another room. "Yes, there he is. He's coming. Mr. Colton," said Witherspoon, with deep impressiveness, "this is my son Henry."

The old man bowed with a politeness in which there was a reminder of a slower and therefore a more courteous day, and taking the hand which Henry cordially offered him, said: "To meet you affects me profoundly, sir. Of course I am acquainted with your early history, and this adds to the interest I feel in you; but aside from this, to meet a son of George Witherspoon must necessarily give me great pleasure."

"Brother Colton is from Maryland," Witherspoon remarked, and a sudden shriveling about the old man's mouth told that he was smiling at what he had long since learned to believe was a capital hit of playfulness. And he bowed, grabbled up a dingy handkerchief that dangled from him somewhere, wiped off his shriveled smile, and then declared that if frankness was a mark of the Marylander, he should always be glad to acknowledge his native State.

Brooks, Colton's son-in-law, now came in. This man, while a floor-walker in a dry-goods store, had attracted Witherspoon's notice, and a position in the Colossus, at that time an experiment, was given him. He recognized the demands of his calling, and he strove to fit himself to them. Several years later he married Miss Colton, and now he was in a position of such confidence that many schemes for the broadening of trade and for the pleasing of the public's changeful fancy were entrusted to his management. He was of a size which appears to set off clothes to the best advantage. His face was pale and thoughtful, and he had the shrewd faculty of knowing when to smile. His eyes were of such a bulge as to give him a spacious range of vision without having to turn his head, and while moving about in the discharge of his duty, he often saw sudden situations that were not intended for his entertainment.

Brooks was prepared for the meeting, and conducted himself with a dignity that would have cast no discredit upon the ablest floor-walker in Christendom. He had known that he could not fail to be impressed by one so closely allied by blood to Mr. George Witherspoon, but really he had not expected to meet a man of so distinguished a bearing, a traveler and a scholar, no doubt.

"Traveler enough to know that I have seen but little, and scholar enough to feel my ignorance," Henry replied.

"Oh, you do yourself an injustice, I am sure, but you do it gracefully. We shall meet often, of course. Mr. Witherspoon," he added, addressing the head of the Colossus, "we have just arrested that Mrs. McNutt."

"How's that? What Mrs. McNutt?"

"Why, the woman who was suspected of shop-lifting. This time we caught her in the act."

"Ah, hah. Have you sent her away?"

"Not yet. She begs for an interview with you—says she can explain everything."

"Don't want to see her; let her explain to the law."

"That's what I told her, sir."

Brooks bowed and withdrew. Old man Colton was already at

his desk.

"Now, my son," said Witherspoon, aimlessly fumbling with some papers on his desk, "I should think that the first thing to be attended to is that statement for the newspapers. Wait a moment, and we will consult Brooks. He knows more in that line than any one else about the place." He tapped a bell. "Mr. Brooks," he said when a boy appeared. Brooks came, and Witherspoon explained.

"Ah, I see," said Brooks. "You don't want to give it to any one paper, for that isn't business. We'll draw off a statement and send it to the City Press Association, and then it will be given out to all the papers."

"That is a capital idea; you will help us get it up."

"Yes, sir," said Brooks, bowing.

"That will not be necessary," Henry protested, unable to disguise his disapproval of the arrangement. "I can write it in a very short time."

"Ah," Witherspoon replied, "but Brooks is used to such work. He writes our advertisements."

"But this isn't an advertisement, and I prefer to write it."

"Of course, if you can do it satisfactorily, but I should think that it would be better if done by a practiced hand."

"I think so too," Henry rejoined, "and for that reason I recommend my own hand. I have worked on newspapers."

"That so? It may be fortunate so far as this one instance is concerned, but as a general thing I shouldn't recommend it.

Newspaper men have such loose methods, as a rule, that they never accomplish much when they turn their attention to business."

Henry laughed, but the merchant had spoken with such seriousness that he was not disposed to turn it off with a show of mirth. His face remained thoughtful, and he said: "We had several newspaper men about here, and not one of them amounted to anything. Brooks, your services will not be needed. In fact, two of them were dishonest," he added, when Brooks had quitted the room. "They were said to be good newspaper men, too. One of them came with 'Journalist' printed on his card; had solicited advertisements for nearly every paper in town. They were all understood to be good solicitors."

"What," said Henry, "were they simply advertising solicitors?"

"Why, yes; and they were said to be good ones."

"But you must know, sir, that an advertising solicitor is not a newspaper man. It makes me sick—I beg your pardon. But it does rile me to hear that one of these fellows has called himself a newspaper man. Of course there are honest and able men in that employment, but they are not to be classed with men whose learning, judgment and strong mental forces make a great newspaper."

So new a life sprang into his voice, and so strong a conviction emphasized his manner, that Witherspoon, for the first time, looked on him with a sort of admiration.

"Well, you seem to be loaded on this subject."

"Yes, but not offensively so, I hope. Now, give me the points you want covered."

"All right; sit here."

Henry took Witherspoon's chair; the merchant walked up and down the room. The points were agreed upon, and the writer was getting well along with his work when Witherspoon suddenly paused in his walk and said to some one outside: "Show him in here."

A pale and restless-looking young man with green neckwear entered the room. "Now, sir," the merchant demanded somewhat sharply, "what do you want with me? You have been here three or four times, I understand. What do you want?"

"We are not alone," the young man answered, glancing at Henry.

"State your business or get out."

"Well, it's rather a delicate matter, sir, and I didn't want anything to do with it, but we don't always have our own way, you know. Er—the editor of the paper"—

"What paper?"

"The *Weekly Call*. The editor sent me with instructions to ask you if this is true?"

He handed a proof-slip to the merchant, and Henry saw Witherspoon's face darken as he read it. The next moment the great merchant stormed: "There isn't a word of truth in it. It is an infamous lie from start to finish."

"I told him I didn't think it was true," said the young man, "but he talked as if he believed it; remarked that you never advertised with him anyway."

"Advertise with him! Why, I didn't know until this minute that such a paper existed. How much of an advertisement does he expect?"

"Hold on a moment!" Henry cried. "Let me kick this fellow into the street."

"Nothing rash," said Witherspoon, putting out his hand. "Sit down, Henry. It will be all right. It's something you don't understand." And speaking to the visitor, he added: "Send me your rates."

"I have them here, sir," he replied, shying out of Henry's reach. He handed a card to Witherspoon.

"Let me see, now. Will half a column for a year be sufficient?"

"Well, that's rather a small ad, sir."

Henry got up again. "I think I'd better kick him into the street."

"No, no; sit down there. Let me manage this. Here." The blackmailer had retreated to the door. "You go back to your editor and tell him that I will put in a column for one year. Wait. Has anybody seen this?" he added, holding up the proof-slip.

"Nobody, sir, and I will have the type distributed as soon as I get back."

"See that you do. Tell Brooks; he will send you the copy.

Now get out. Infamous scoundrel!" he said when the fellow was gone. "But don't say anything about it at home, for it really amounts to nothing."

He tore the proof-slip into small fragments and threw them into the spittoon.

"What is it all about?" Henry asked.

"Oh, it's the foulest of fabrication. About a year ago there came a widow from Washington with a letter from one of our friends, and asked for a position in the store. Well, we gave her employment, and—and it is about her; but it really amounts to nothing."

"Why, then, didn't you let me kick the scoundrel into the street?"

"My dear boy, to a man who has the money it is easier to pay than to explain. The public is greedy for scandal, but looks with suspicion and coldness upon a correction. One is sweet; the other is tasteless. The rapid acquisition of wealth is associated with some mysterious crime, and men who have failed in wild speculations are the first to cry out against the millionaire. The rich man must pay for the privilege of being rich."

The statement was sent to the city press. It reminded the public of the abduction of Henry Witherspoon; touched upon the sensation created at the time, and upon the long season of interest that had followed; explained the part which the uncle had played, and delicately gave his cause for playing it. And the return of the wanderer was set forth with graphic directness.

At noon the merchant and Henry ate luncheon in a club

where thick rugs hushed a foot-fall into a mere whisper of a walk, where servants, grave of countenance and low of voice, seemed to underscore the chilliness of the place. Henry was introduced to a number of astonished men, who said that they welcomed him home, and who immediately began to talk about something else; and he was shown through the large library, where a solitary man sat looking at the pictures in a comic weekly. After leaving the club they went to a tailor's shop, and then drove over the boulevards and through the parks. Witherspoon, with no pronounced degree of pride, had conducted Henry through the Colossus; he had been pleased, of course, at the young man's astonishment, and he must have been moved by a strong surge of self-glorification when his son wondered at the broadness of the Witherspoon empire, yet he had held in a strong subjection all signs of an unseemly pride. But when he struck the boulevard system, his dignified reserve went to pieces.

"Finest on earth; no doubt about that. Oh, of course, many years of talk and thousands of pages of print have paved the Paris boulevards with peculiar interest, but wipe out association, and where would they be in comparison with these? Look at that stretch. And a few years ago this land could have been picked up for almost nothing. Look at those flowers."

It was now past midsummmer, but no suggestion of a coming blight lay upon the flower-beds. "Look at those trees. Why, in time they will knock the New Haven elms completely out."

CHAPTER IX

THE INTERVIEWERS

When they reached home at evening they found that five reporters had been shown into the library and were waiting for them.

"Glad to see you, gentlemen," said Witherspoon, smiling in his way of pleasant dismissal, "but really that statement contains all that it is necessary for the public to know. We don't want to make a sensation of it, you understand."

"Of course not," one of the newspaper men replied.

"And," said the merchant, with another smile, "I don't know what else can be said."

But the smile had missed its aim. The attention of the visitors was settled upon Henry. There was no chance for separate interviews, and questions were asked by first one and then another.

"You had no idea that your parents were alive?"

"Not until after my uncle's death."

"Had he ever told you why you were in his charge?"

"Yes; he said that at the death of my parents I had been given to him."

"You of course knew the story of the mysterious disappearance of Henry Witherspoon."

"Yes; when a boy I had read something about it."

"In view of the many frauds that had been attempted, hadn't you a fear that your father might he suspicious of you?"

"No; I had forwarded letters and held proof that could not be disputed. The mystery was cleared up."

"How old are you?"

"I shall be twenty-five next—next"—

"December the fourteenth," Witherspoon answered for him.

"The truth is," said Henry, "uncle did not remember the exact date of my birth."

"Was your uncle a man of means?"

"Well, I can hardly say that he was. He speculated considerably, and though he was never largely successful, yet he always managed to live well."

"Were you engaged in any sort of employment?"

"Yes, at different times I was a reporter."

"It is not necessary that the public should know all this,"

said Witherspoon.

"But we can't help it," Henry replied. "The statement we sent out would simply serve to hone and strap public curiosity to a keen edge. I expected something of this sort. The only thing to do is to get through with it as soon as we can."

When the interview was ended Henry went to the front door with the reporters, and at parting said to them: "I hope to see you again, gentlemen, and doubtless I shall. I am one of you."

At dinner that evening Witherspoon was in high spirits. He joked—a recreation rare with him—and he told a story—a mental excursion of marked uncommonness.

"What, Henry, don't you drink wine at all?" the merchant asked.

"No, sir, I stand in mortal fear of it." The vision of a drunken painter, he always fancied, hung like a fog between him and the liquor glass.

"It's well enough, my son."

"None of the Craigs were drunkards," said Ellen, giggling.

"Ellen," Mrs. Witherspoon solemnly enjoined, "my mother's people shall not be made sport of. It is true that there were no drunkards among them. And why?"

"Because none of them got drunk, I should think," Henry ventured to suggest.

"That, of course, was one reason, my son, but the main reason was that they knew how to govern themselves."

The evening flew away with music and with talk of a long ago made doubly dear by present happiness. The hour was growing late. Witherspoon and Henry sat in the library, smoking. Ellen had gone to her room to draft a form for the invitation to Henry's reception, and Mrs. Witherspoon was on a midnight prowl throughout the house, and although knowing that everything was right, yet surprised to find it so.

"Now, my boy," said the merchant, "we will talk business. Your mother, and particularly your sister, thought it well for me to make you an allowance, and while I don't object to the putting of money aside for you, yet I should rather have you feel the manliness which comes of drawing a salary for services rendered. That is more American. You see how useful Brooks has made himself. Now, why can't you work yourself into a similar position? In the future, the charge of the entire establishment may devolve upon you. All that a real man wants is a chance, and such a chance as I now urge upon you falls to the lot of but few young men. Had such an opportunity been given to me when I was young, I should have regarded myself as one specially favored by the partial goddess of fortune."

He was now walking up and down the room. He spoke with fervor, and Henry saw how strong he was and wondered not at his great success.

"I don't often resort to figures of speech," Witherspoon continued, "but even the most practical man feels sometimes that illustration is a necessity. Words are the trademarks of the goods stored in the mind, and a flashy expression proclaims the flimsy trinket."

Was his unwonted indulgence in wine at dinner playing rhetorical tricks with his mind?

"I spoke just now of the partial goddess of fortune," the merchant continued, "in the hope that I might impress you with a deplorable truth. Fortune is vested with a peculiar discrimination. It appears more often to favor the unjust than the just. Ability and a life of constant wooing do not always win success, for luck, the factotum of fortune, often bestows in one minute a success which a life-time of stubborn toil could not have achieved. Therefore, I say to you, think well of your position, and instead of drawing idly upon your great advantage, add to it. Successful men are often niggardly of advice, while the prattling tongue nearly always belongs to failure; therefore, when a successful man does advise, heed him. I think that I should have succeeded in nearly any walk of life. Sturdy New England stock, the hard necessity for thrift, and the practical common school fitted me to push my way to the front. Don't think that I am boasting. It is no more of vanity for one to say 'I have succeeded' than to say 'I will succeed.'" He paused a moment and stood near Henry's chair. "You have the chance to become what I cannot be—one of the wealthiest men in this country." He sat down, and leaning back in his leather-covered chair, stretched forth his legs and crossed his slippered feet. He looked at Henry.

"To some men success is natural, and to others it is impossible," Henry replied. "I can well see that prosperity could not long have kept beyond your reach. Your mind led you in a certain direction, and instead of resisting, you gladly followed it. You say that you should have been a success in any walk of life, and while it is true that you would have made money, it does not follow that you would have found that contentment which is beyond all earthly price. I admit that the opportunity which you offer me is one of rarest advantage, but knowing myself, I feel that in accepting it I should be doing you an injustice. It may be so strange to you that you can't understand it, yet I haven't a single commercial instinct; and to be frank with you, that great store would be a penitentiary to me. Wait a moment." Witherspoon had bounded to his feet. "I am willing to do almost anything," Henry continued, "but I can't consent to a complete darkening of my life. I admit that I am peculiar, and shall not dispute you in your belief that my mind is not strong, but I am firm when it comes to purpose. To hear one say that he doesn't care to be the richest man in the country may strike you as the utterance of a fool, and yet I am compelled to say it. I don't want you to make me an allowance. I don't want"—

"What in God's name do you want, sir!" Witherspoon exclaimed. He was walking up and down the room, not with the regular paces which had marked his stroll a few moments before, but with the uneven tread of anger. "What in God's name can you ask?"

He turned upon Henry, and standing still, gave him a look of hard inquiry.

"I ask nothing in God's name, and surely nothing in my own. I knew that this would put you out, and I dreaded it, but it had to come. Suppose that at my age the opportunity to manage a cattle ranch had been offered you."

"I would have taken it; I would have made it the biggest cattle ranch in the country. It galls me, sir, it galls me to see my own children sticking up their noses at honest employment."

"Pardon me, but so far as I am concerned you are wrong. I seek honest employment. But what is the most honest employment? Any employment that yields an income? No; but the work that one is best fitted for and which is therefore the most satisfactory. If you had shaped my early life"—

"Andrew was a fool!" Witherspoon broke in. "He was crazy."

"But he was something of a gentleman, sir."

"Gentleman!" Witherspoon snorted; "he was the worst of all thieves—a child-stealer."

"And had you been entirely blameless, sir?"

"What! and do you reproach me? Now look here." He pointed a shaking finger at Henry. "Don't you ever hint at such a thing again. My God, this is disgraceful!" he muttered, resuming his uneven walk. "My hopes were so built up. Now you knock them down. What the devil do you want, sir!" he exclaimed, wheeling about.

"I will tell you if you will listen."

"Oh, yes, of course you will. It will no doubt do you great good to humiliate me."

"When you feel, sir, that I am humiliating you, one word is all you need to say."

"What's that? Come now, no foolish threats. What is it you want to do?"

"I have an idea," Henry answered, "that I could manage a newspaper."

"The devil you have."

"Yes, the devil I have, if you insist. I am a newspaper man and I like the work. It holds a fascination for me while everything else is dull. Now, I have a proposal to make, not a modest one, perhaps, but one which I hope you will patiently consider—if you can. It would be easy for you to get control of some afternoon newspaper. I can take charge of it, and in time pay back the money you invest. I don't ask you to give me a cent."

The merchant was about to reply, when Mrs. Witherspoon entered the room. "Why, what is the matter?" she asked.

Witherspoon resumed his seat, shoved his hands deep into his pockets, stretched forth his legs, crossed his feet and nervously shook them.

"What is the matter?" she repeated.

"Everything's the matter," Witherspoon declared. "I have suggested"—he didn't say demanded—"that Henry should go into the store and gradually take charge of the whole thing, and he positively refuses. He wants to ran a newspaper." The merchant grunted and shook his feet.

"But is there anything so bad about that?" she asked. "I am sure it is no more than natural. My uncle Louis used to write for the Salem *Monitor*."

He looked at her—he did not say a word, but he looked at her.

"And Uncle Harvey"—

He grunted, flounced out of his chair and quitted the room.

"Mother," said Henry, getting up and taking her hand, "I am grieved that this dispute arose. I know that he is set in his ways, and it is unfortunate that I was compelled to cross him, but it had to come sooner or later."

"I am very sorry, but I don't blame you, my son. If you don't want to go into the store, why should you?"

They heard Witherspoon's jolting walk, up and down the hall.

"You have but one life here on this earth," she said, "and I don't see why you should make that one life miserable by engaging in something that is distasteful to you. But if your father has a fault it is that he believes every one should think as he does. Don't say anything more to him to-night."

When Henry went out Witherspoon was still walking up and down the hall. They passed, but took not the slightest notice of each other. How different from the night before. Henry lay awake, thinking of the dead boy, and pictured his eternal sleeping-place, hard by the stormy sea.

CHAPTER X

ROMPED WITH THE GIRL

The morning was heavy and almost breathless. The smoke of the city hung low in the streets. Henry had passed through a dreamful and uneasy sleep. He thought it wise to remain in his room until the merchant was gone down town, and troublously he had begun to doze again when Ellen's voice aroused him. "Come on down!" she cried, tapping on the door. "You just ought to see what the newspapers have said about you. Everybody in the neighborhood is staring at us. Come on down."

Witherspoon was sitting on a sofa with a pile of newspapers beside him. He looked up as Henry entered, and in the expression of his face there was no displeasure to recall the controversy of the night before.

"Well, sir," said he, "they have given you a broad spread."

The reporters had done their work well. It was a great sensation. Henry was variously described. One report said that he had a dreaminess of eye that was not characteristic of this strong, pragmatic family; another declared him to be "tall, rather handsome, black-bearded, and with the quiet sense of humor that belongs to the temperament of a modest

Opie Read

man." One reporter had noticed that his Southern-cut clothes did not fit him.

"He might have said something nicer than that," Ellen remarked, with a natural protest against this undue familiarity.

"I don't know why we should be spoken of as a pragmatic family," said Mrs. Witherspoon. "Of course your father has always been in business, but I don't see"—

Witherspoon began to grunt. "It's all right," said he. "It's all right." He had to say something. "Come, I must get down town."

"Shall I go with you?" Henry asked.

For a moment Witherspoon was silent. "Not unless you want to," he answered.

They sat down to breakfast. Henry nervously expected another outbreak. The merchant began to say something, but stopped on a half utterance and cleared his throat. "It is coming," Henry thought.

"I have studied over our talk of last night," said Witherspoon, "and while I won't say that you may be right, or have any excuse for presuming that you are right, I am inclined to indulge that wild scheme of yours for a while. My impression is that you'll soon get sick of it."

Mrs. Witherspoon looked at him thankfully. "And you will give him a chance, father," she said.

"Didn't I say I would? Isn't that exactly what I said? Gracious alive, don't make me out a grinding and unyielding monster. We'll look round, Henry, and see what can be done. Brooks may know of some opening. You'd better rest here to-day."

"I am deeply grateful, sir, for the concession you have made," Henry replied. "I know how you feel on the subject, and I regret"—

"All right."

"Regret that I was forced"—

"I said it was all right."

"Forced to oppose you, but I don't think that you'll have cause to feel ashamed of me."

"You have already made me feel proud of your manliness," said Witherspoon.

Henry bowed, and Mrs. Witherspoon gave her husband an impulsive look of gratitude. The merchant continued:

"You have refused my offer, but you have not presumed upon your own position. Sincerity expects a reward, as a rule, and when a man is sincere at his own expense, there is something about him to admire. You don't prefer to live idly—to draw on me—and I should want no stronger proof that you are, indeed, my son. It is stronger than the gold chain you brought home with you, for that might have been found; but manly traits are not to be picked up; they come of inheritance. Well, I must go. I will speak to Brooks and see if anything can be done."

Rain began to fall. How full of restful meditation was this dripping-time, how brooding with half-formed, languorous thoughts that begin as an idea and end as a reverie. Sometimes a soothing spirit which the sun could not evoke

Opie Read

from its boundless fields of light comes out of the dark bosom of a cloud. A bright day promises so much, so builds our hopes, that our keenest disappointments seem to come on a radiant morning, but on a dismal day, when nothing has been promised, a straggling pleasure is accidentally found and is pressed the closer to the senses because it was so unexpected.

To Henry came the conviction that he was doing his duty, and yet he could not at times subdue the feeling that pleasant environment was the advocate that had urged this decision. But he refused to argue with himself. Sometimes he strode after Mrs. Witherspoon as she went about the house, and he knew that she was happy because be followed her; and up and down the hall he romped with Ellen. They termed it a frolic that they should have enjoyed years ago, and they laughingly said that from the past they would snatch their separated childhood and blend it now. It was a back-number pleasure, they agreed, but that, like an old print, it held a charm in its quaintness. She brought out a doll that had for years been asleep in a little blue trunk. "Her name is Rose," she said, and with a broad ribbon she deftly made a cap and put it on the doll's head. After a while Rose was put to sleep again—the bright little mummy of a child's affection, Henry called her—and the playmates became older. She told him of the many suitors that had sought to woo her; of rich men; of poor young fellows who strove to keep time to the quick-changing tune of fashion; of moon-impressed youths who measured their impatient yearning.

"And when are you going to let one of them take you away?" Henry asked. Holding his hand, she had led him in front of a mirror.

"Oh, not at all," she answered, smiling at herself and then at him. "I haven't fallen in love with anybody yet."

"And is that necessary?"

"Why, you know it is, goose. I'd be a pretty-looking thing to marry a man I didn't love, wouldn't I?"

"You are a pretty thing anyway."

"Oh, do you really think so?"

"I know it."

"You are making fun of me. If you had met me accidentally, would you have thought so?"

"Surely; my eyes are always open to the truth."

"If I could meet such a man as you are I could love him—'with a dreaminess of eye not characteristic of this strong, pragmatic family.'"

She broke away from him, but he caught her. "If I were not related to you," he said, "I would be tempted to kiss you."

"Oh, you'd be *tempted* to kiss me, would you? If you were not related to me I wouldn't let you, but as it is—there!"

His blood tingled. Her hair was falling about her shoulders. For a moment it was a strife for him to believe that she was his sister.

"Beautiful," he said, running his fingers through her hair. "Somebody said that the glory of a woman is her hair; and it is true. It is a glory that always catches me."

"Does it? Well, I must put up my glory before papa comes. Oh, you are such a romp; but I was just a little afraid of you at first, you were so sedate and dreamy of eye."

She ran away from him, and looking back with mischief in her eyes, she hummed a schottish, and keeping time to it, danced up the stairway.

When Witherspoon came to dinner he said that he had consulted Brooks and that the resourceful manager knew of a possible opening.

The owner of the *Star*, a politician who had been foolish enough to suppose that with the control of an editorial page he could illumine his virtues and throw darkness over his faults, was willing to part with his experiment. "I think that we can get it at a very reasonable figure," said Witherspoon. And after a moment's silence he added: "Brooks can pull you a good many advertisements in a quiet way, and possibly the thing may be made to turn oat all right. But I tell you again that I am very much disappointed. Your place is with me— but we won't talk about it. How came you to take up that line of work?"

"I began by selling newspapers."

Mrs. Witherspoon sighed, and the merchant asked: "And did Andrew urge it?"

"Oh, no. In fact I was a reporter before he knew anything about it."

Witherspoon grunted. "I should have thought," said he, "that your uncle would have looked after you with more care. Did you receive a regular course of training?" Henry looked at him. "At school, I mean."

"Yes, in an elementary way. Afterward I studied in the

public library."

"A good school, but not cohesive," Witherspoon replied. "A thousand scraps of knowledge don't make an education."

"Father, you remember my uncle Harvey," said Mrs. Witherspoon.

"Hum, yes, I remember him."

"Well, his education did not prevent his having a thousand scraps of knowledge."

"I should think not," Witherspoon replied. "No man's knowledge interferes with his education."

"My uncle Harvey knew nearly everything," Mrs. Witherspoon went on. "He could make a clock; and he was one of the best school teachers in the country. I shouldn't think that education consists in committing a few rules to memory."

"No, Caroline, not in the committing of a thousand rules to memory, but without rule there is no complete education."

"I shouldn't think that there could be a complete education anyway," she rejoined, in a tone which Henry knew was meant in defense of himself.

"Of course not," said the merchant, and turning from the subject as from something that could interest him but little, he again took up the newspaper project. "We'll investigate that matter to-morrow, and if you are still determined to go into it, the sooner the better. My own opinion is that you will soon get tired of it, in view of the better advantages that I urge upon you, for the worries of an experimental concern will serve to strengthen my proposal."

"I am resolved that in the end it shall cost you nothing," Henry replied.

"Hum, we'll see about that. But whatever you do, do it earnestly, for a failure in one line does not argue success in another direction. In business it is well to beware of men who have failed. They bring bad luck. Without success there may be vanity, but there can be but little pride, little self-respect."

Henry moved uneasily in his chair. "But among those who have failed," he replied, "we often find the highest types of manhood."

"Nonsense," rejoined the merchant. "That is merely a poetic idea. What do you mean by the highest type of manhood? Men whose theories have all been proved to be wrong? Great men have an aim and accomplish it. America is a great country, and why? Because it is prosperous."

"I don't mean that failure necessarily implies that a man's aim has been high," said Henry, "neither do I think that financial success is greatness. But our views are at variance and I fear that we shall never be able to reconcile them. I may be wrong, and it is more than likely that I am. At times I feel that there is nothing in the entire scheme of life. If a man is too serious we call him a pessimist; if he is too happy we know that he is an idiot."

"Henry, you are too young a man to talk that way."

"My son," said Mrs. Witherspoon, "the Lord has made us for a special purpose, and we ought not to question His plans."

"No, mother," Ellen spoke up, "but we should like to know something about that especial part of the plan which relates to us."

"My daughter, this is not a question for you to discuss. Your duty in this life is so clearly marked out that there can be no mistake about it. With my son it has unfortunately been different."

The girl smiled. "A woman's duty is not so clearly marked out now as it used to be, mother. As long as man was permitted to mark it out her duty was clear enough—to him."

"Hum!" Witherspoon grunted, "we are about to have a woman's advancement session. Will you please preside?" he added, nodding at Ellen. She laughed at him. He continued: "After a while Vassar will be nothing but a woman's convention. Henry, we will go down to-morrow and look after that newspaper."

CHAPTER XI

ACKNOWLEDGED BY SOCIETY

The politician was surprised. He had not supposed that any one even suspected that he wanted to get rid of the *Star*; indeed, he was not aware that the public knew of his ownership of that paper. It was a very valuable piece of property; but unfortunately his time was so taken up with other matters that he could not give it the attention it deserved. Its circulation was growing every day, and with proper management its influence could be extended to every corner of the country. Witherspoon replied that he was surprised to hear that the paper was doing so well. He did not often see a copy of it. The politician and the merchant understood each other, and the bargain was soon brought to a close.

And now the time for the reception was at hand. A florist's wagon stood in front of the door, and the young man thought, "This is my funeral." Every preparation gave him a shudder. Ellen laughed at him.

"It's well enough for you to laugh," said he, "for you are safe in the amphitheater while I am in the ring with the bull."

"Why, you great big goose, is anybody going to hurt you?"

"No; and that's the trouble. If somebody were to hurt me, I could relieve myself of embarrassment by taking up revenge."

At the very eleventh hour of preparation he was not only reconciled to the affliction of a reception, but appeared rather to look with favor upon the affair. And it was this peculiar reasoning that brought him round: "I am here in place of another. I am not known. I am as a writer who hides behind a pen-name."

The evening came with a rumble of carriages. An invitation to a reception means, "Come and be pleased. Frowns are to be left at home." The difference between one society gathering and another is the difference that exists between two white shoes—one may be larger than the other. Witherspoon was lordly, and in his smile a stranger might have seen a life of generosities. And with what a welcoming dignity he took the hand that in its time had cut the throats of a thousand hogs. Diamonds gleamed in the mellowed light, and there were smiles none the less radiant for having been carefully trained. The evening was warm. There was a wing-like movement of feathered fans. Scented time was flying away.

The guests were gone, and Henry sat in his room. He had thrown off the garments which convention had prescribed, and now, with his feet on a table, he sat smoking an old black pipe that he had lolled with on the mountains of Costa Rica. The night which was now ending waved back for review. Ellen, beautiful in an empire gown, golden yellow, brocaded satin. "Why did you try to dodge this?" she had asked in a whisper. "You are the most self-possessed man in the house. Can't you see how proud we all are of you? I have never seen mother so happy."

Opie Read

The perfume of praise was in the air. "Oh, I think your brother is just charming," a young woman had said to Ellen, and Henry had caught the words.

"He is like my mother's people." Mrs. Witherspoon was talking to a woman whose hair had been grayed and who appeared to enjoy the distinction of being an invalid. The Coltons and the Brooks contingent had smeared him with compliments. There was a literary group, and the titles of a hundred books were mentioned; one writer was charming; another was horrid. There was the group of household government, and the servant-girl question, which has never been found in repose, was tossed from one woman to another and caught as a bag of sweets. In the library was a commercial and real-estate gathering, and the field of speculation was broken up, harrowed and seeded down.

The black-bearded muser put his pipe aside, and from this glowing scene his thoughts flew away into a dark night when he stood in Ulmata, knocking at the door of a deserted house. He got up and stood at the window. Sparrows twittered. Threads of gray dawn streaked the black warp of night.

At morning there was another spread in the newspapers. The wonder of a few days had spent its force, and the Witherspoon sensation was done.

CHAPTER XII

A DEMOCRACY

The *Star* was printed in an old building where more than one newspaper had failed. The interior of the place was so comfortless in arrangement, so subject to unaccountable drafts of cold air in winter and breaths of hot oppression in summer, that it must have been built especially for a newspaper office. Henry found that the working force consisted mainly of a few young reporters and a large force of editorial writers. The weakness of nearly every newspaper is its editorial page, and especially so when the paper is owned by a politician. The new manager straightway began a reorganization. It was an easy matter to form an efficient staff, for in every city some of the best newspaper men are out of employment—the bright and uncertain writers who have been shoved aside by trustworthy plodders. He did not begin as one who knows it all, but he sought the co-operation of practical men. The very man who knew that the paper could not do without him was told that his services were no longer needed. In his day he had spread many an acre of platitudes; he had hammered the tariff mummy, and at every lick he had knocked out the black dust; he had snorted loud in controversy, and was arrogant in the certainty that his blowhard sentence was the frosty air of satire. He was the representative of a class. To him all clearness of expression was shallowness of thought, and brightness was the essence of frivolity. He soon found another place, for some of the Chicago newspapers still set a premium upon windy dullness.

Among the writers whom Henry decided to retain was Laura Drury. She wrote book reviews and scraps which were supposed to be of interest to women. Her room opened into Henry's, and through a door which was never shut he could see her at work. The brightness and the modesty of her face attracted him. She could not have been more than twenty years of age.

"Have you been long in newspaper work?" he asked, when she had come in to submit something to him.

"Only a short time," she answered, and returned at once to her desk. Henry looked at her as she proceeded with her work. Her presence seemed to refine the entire office. He fancied that her hair made the room brighter. His curiosity was awakened by one touch of her presence. He sought to know more of her, and when she had come in again to consult him, he said: "Wait a moment, please. How long have you been connected with this paper?"

"About three months, regularly."

"Had you worked on any other paper in the city?"

"No, sir; I have never worked on any other paper."

"Have you lived here long?"

"No, sir, I have been here only a short time. I am from Missouri."

"You didn't come alone, did you?"

She glanced at him quickly and answered: "I came alone, but I live with my aunt."

She returned to her work, and she must have discovered that he was watching her, for the next day he saw that she had moved her desk.

Henry had applied for membership in the Press Club, and one morning a reporter told him that he had been elected.

"Was there any opposition?" the editor asked.

"Not after the boys learned that you had been a reporter. You can go over at any time and sign the constitution."

"I'll go now. Suppose you come with me."

The Press Club of Chicago is a democracy. Money holds but little influence within its precincts, for its ablest members are generally "broke." There are no rules hung on its walls, no cool ceremonies to be observed. Its atmosphere invites a man to be natural, and warns him to conceal his vanities. Among that body of men no pretense is sacred. Here men of Puritan ancestry find it well to curb a puritanical instinct. A stranger may be shocked by a snort of profanity, but if he listens he will hear a bright and poetic blending of words rippling after it. A great preacher, whose sermons are read by the world, sat one day in the club, uttering the slow and heavy sentences of an oracle. He touched his finger tips together. He was discoursing on some phase of life; and an old night police reporter listened for a moment and said, "Rats!" The great man was startled. Accustomed to deliver his theories to a silent congregation, he was astonished to find that his wisdom could so irreverently be questioned. The reporter meant no disrespect, but he could not restrain his contempt for so presuming a piece of ignorance. He turned to the preacher and showed him where his theories were wrong. With a pin he touched the bubble of the great man's presumption, and it was done kindly, for when the sage arose to go he said: "I must confess that I have learned something. I fear that a preacher's library does not contain all that is worth knowing." And this, more than any of his sermons, proved his wisdom.

In the Press Club the pulse of the town can be felt, and scandals that money and social influence have suppressed are known there. The characters of public men are correctly estimated; snobs are laughed at; and the society woman who seeks to bribe the press with she cajolery of a smile is a familiar joke. Of course this is not wholly a harmonious body, for keen intelligence is never in smooth accord with itself. To the "kicker" is given the right to "kick," and keen is the enjoyment of this privilege. Every directory is the worst; every officer neglects his duty.

Literary societies know but little of this club, for literary societies despise the affairs of the real worker—they are interested in the bladdery essay written by the fashionable ass.

Henry was shown into a large room, brightly carpeted and hung with portraits. On a leather lounge a man lay asleep; at a round table a man sat, solemnly playing solitaire; and in one corner of the apartment sat several men, discussing an outrageous clause in the constitution that Henry had just signed. The new member was introduced to them. Among the number were John McGlenn, John Richmond and a shrewd little Yankee named Whittlesy. Of McGlenn's character a whole book might be written. An individual almost wholly distinct from his fellow-men; a castigator of human weakness and yet a hero-worshiper—not the hero of burning powder and fluttering flags, but any human being whose brain had blazed and lighted the world. Art was to him the soul of literature. Had he lived two thousand years ago, as the founder of a peculiar school of philosophy, he might still be alive. If frankness be a virtue, he was surely a reward unto himself. He would calmly look into the eyes of a poet and say, "Yes, I read your poem. Do you expect to keep on attempting to write poetry? But you may think better of it after a while. I wrote poems when I was of your age." He did not hate men because they were wealthy, but he despised the methods that make them rich. His temperament invited a few people to a close friendship with him, and gently warned many to keep a respectful distance. Aggressive and cutting he was, and he often said that death was the best friend of a man who is compelled to write for a living. He wrote a subscription book for a mere pittance, and one of the agents that sold it now lives in a mansion. He regarded present success as nothing to compare with an immortal name in the ages to come. He was born in the country, and his refined nature revolted at his rude surroundings, and ever afterward he held the country in contempt. In later years he had regarded himself simply as a man of talent, and when this decision had been reached he thought less of life. If his intellectual character lacked one touch, that touch would have made him a genius. When applied to him the term "gentleman" found its befitting place.

Careless observers of men often passed Richmond without taking particular notice of him. He was rather undersized, and was bald, but his head was shapely. He was so sensitive that he often assumed a brusqueness in order not to appear effeminate. His judgment of men was as swift as the sweep of a hawk, and sometimes it was as sure. He had taken so many chances, and had so closely noted that something which we call luck, that he might have been touched a little

Opie Read

with superstition, but his soul was as broad as a prairie, and his mind was as penetrating as a drill; and a fact must have selected a close hiding-place to escape his search. Sitting in his room, with his plug of black tobacco, he had explored the world. Stanley was amazed at his knowledge of Africa, and Blaine marveled at his acquaintance with political history.

"We welcome you to our club," McGlenn remarked when Henry had sat down, "but are you sure that this is the club you wanted to join!"

Henry was surprised. "Of course I am. Why do you ask that question?"

"Because you are a rich man, and this is the home of modesty."

Henry reached over and shook hands with him. "I like that," said he, "and let me assure you that you have in one sentence made me feel that I really belong here, not because I am particularly modest, but because your sentiments are my own. I am not a rich man, but even if I were I should prefer this group to the hyphenated"—

"Fools," McGlenn suggested.

"Yes," Henry agreed, "the hyphenated fools that I am compelled to meet. George Witherspoon is a rich man, but his money does not belong to me. I didn't help him earn any of it; I borrowed money from him, and, so soon as I can, I shall return it with interest."

"John," said Richmond, "you were wrong—as you usually are—in asking Mr. Witherspoon that question, but in view of the fact that you enabled him to put himself so agreeably on record, we will excuse your lack of courtesy."

"I don't permit any man who goes fishing with any sort of ignorant lout, and who spends a whole day in a boat with him, to tell me when I am lacking in courtesy."

Richmond laughed, put his hand to his mouth, threw back his head and replied: "I go fishing, not for society, but for amusement; and, by the way, I think it would do you good to go fishing, even with an ignorant lout. You might learn something."

"Ah," McGlenn rejoined, "you have disclosed the source of much of your information. You learn from the ignorant that you may confound the wise."

Richmond put his hand to his mouth. "At some playful time," said he, "I might seek to confound the wise, but I should never so far forget myself as to make an experiment on you."

"Mr. Witherspoon," remarked McGlenn, "we will turn from this rude barbarian and give our attention to Mr. Whittlesy, who knows all about dogs."

"If he knows all about dogs," Henry replied, "he must be well acquainted with some of the most prominent traits of man."

"I am not talking much to-day," said Whittlesy, ducking his head. "I went fooling round the Board of Trade yesterday; and they got me, and they got me good."

"How much did they catch you for, Whit?" McGlenn asked.

"I won't say, but they got me, and got me good, but never mind. Ill go after 'em."

The man who had been asleep on the leather lounge got up,

stretched himself, looked about for a moment, and then, coming over to the group, said: "What's all this bloody rot?" Seeing a stranger, he added, by way of apology: "I thought this was the regular roasting lay-out."

"Mr. Witherspoon," said Richmond, "let me introduce Mr. Mortimer, an old member of the club;" and when the introduction had been acknowledged, Richmond added: "Mortimer has just thought of something mean to say and has come over to say it. He dozes himself full of venom and then has to get rid of it."

"Our friend Richmond is about as truthful as he is complimentary," Mortimer replied.

"Yes," said Richmond, "but if I were no more complimentary than you are truthful, I should have a slam for everybody."

"Oh, ho, ho, no," McGlenn cried, and Richmond shouted: "Oh, I have been robbed."

Henry looked about for the cause of this commotion and saw a smiling man, portly and impressive, coming toward them with a dignified mince in his walk. And Mr. Flummers was introduced with half-humorous ceremony. He had rather a pleasant expression of countenance, and men who were well acquainted with him said that he had, though not so long of arm, an extensive reach for whisky. He was of impressive size, with a sort of Napoleonic head; and when hot on the trail of a drink, his voice held a most unctuous solicitude. He was exceedingly annoying to some people and was a source of constant delight to others. At one time he had formed the habit of being robbed, and later on he was drugged; but no one could conjecture what he would next add to his repertory. His troubles were amusing, his difficulties were humorous, his failures were laughable, and his sorrows were the cause for jest. He had a growing paunch, and when he stood he leaned back slightly as though his rotund front found ease in exhibition. As a law student he had aimed a severe blow at justice, and failing as an attorney, he had served his country a good turn. As a reporter he wrote with a torch, and wrote well. All his utterances were declamatory; and he had a set of scallopy gestures that were far beyond the successful mimicry of his fellows. The less he thought the more wisely he talked. Meditation hampered him, and like a rabbit, he was generally at his best when he first "jumped up."

He shook hands with Henry, looked at him a moment and asked: "Are you going to run a newspaper with all those old geysers you've got over there?"

The new member winced.

"Don't pay any attention to Flummers," John Richmond said.

"Oh, yes," Flummers insisted. "You see, I know all those fellows. Some of them were worn out ten years ago—but say, are you paying anything over there?"

"Yes, paying as much as any paper in the town."

"That's the stuff; but say, you can afford it. Who rang the bell? Did anybody ring? Boy," (speaking to a waiter), "we ought to have something to drink here."

"Do *you* want to pay for it?" Richmond asked.

"Oh, ho, ho, no, I'm busted. I've set 'em up two or three times to-day."

"Why, you stuffed buffalo robe, you"—

"Oh, well, it was the other day, then. I'm all the time buying the drinks. If it weren't for me you geysers would dry up. Say, John, touch the bell."

"Wait," said Henry. "Have something with me."

"Ah, now you command the respect of the commonwealth!" Flummers cried. "By one heroic act you prove that your life is not a failure. These fellows round here make me tired. Boy, bring me a little whisky. What are you fellows going to take? What! you want a cigar?" he added, speaking to Henry.

"Oh, I had a great man on my staff yesterday—big railroad man. Do you know that some of those fellows like to have a man show them how to spend their money? I see I'm posted for dues. This municipality must think I'm made of money."

When he caught sight of the boy coming with the tray, a peculiar light, such as painters give the face of Hope, illumined his countenance, and clasping his hands, he unctuously greeted himself.

"Mr. Flummers," said McGlenn, "we all love you."

"Oh, no."

"Yes; it is disreputable, but we love you. It was a long time before I discovered your beauties. I used to think that the men who loved you were the enemies of a higher grade of life, and perhaps they were, but I love you. You are a great man, Mr. Flummers. Nature designed you to be the president of a life insurance company."

"Well, say, I know that."

"Yes," continued McGlenn. "A life insurance company ought

to employ you as a great joss, and charge people for the privilege of a mere glimpse of you."

"I shouldn't think," said Richmond, "that a man who had committed murder in Nebraska would be so extreme as to pose as the president of a life insurance company."

"Mr. Hammers, did you commit a murder in Nebraska?" McGlenn asked.

"Oh, no."

"But didn't you confess that you killed a man there?" Richmond urged.

"Oh, well, that was a mistake."

"What? The confession?"

"No, the killing. You see, I was out of work, and I struck a doctor for a job in his drug-store; and once, when the doctor was away, an old fellow sent over to have a prescription filled, and I filled it. And when the doctor returned he saw the funeral procession going past the store. He asked me what it meant, and I told him."

"Then what did he say?"

"He asked me if I got pay for the prescription. Oh, but he was a thrifty man!" Flummers clasped his hands, threw himself back and laughed with a jolting "he, he, he." "Well, I've got to go. Did anybody ring? Say, John"—to Richmond—"why don't you buy something?"

"What? Oh, you gulp, you succession of swallows, you human sink-hole! Flummers, I have bought you whisky enough to overflow the Mississippi."

"Oh, ho, ho, but not to-day, John. Past whisky is a scandal; in present whisky there lies a virtue. Never tell a man what you have done, John, lest he may think you boastful, but show him what you will do now, so that he may have the proof of your ability. Is it possible that I've got to shake you fellows? My time is too valuable to waste even with a mere contemplation of your riotous living."

He walked away with his mincing step. "There's a character," said Henry, looking after him. "He is positively restful."

"Until he wants a drink," Mortimer replied, "and then he is restless. Well, I must follow his example of withdrawal, if not his precept of appetite. I am pleased to have met you, Mr. Witherspoon, and I hope to see you often."

"I think you shall, as I intend to make this my resting-place."

"There is another character," said McGlenn, referring to Mortimer. "He is a very learned man, so much so that he has no need of imagination. He is a *very* learned man."

"And he is charmed with the prospect of saying a mean thing," Richmond replied. "I tell him so," he added, "though that is needless, for he knows it himself. His mind has traveled over a large scope of intellectual territory, and he commands my respect while I object to his methods."

The conversation took a serious turn, and Richmond flooded it with his learning. His voice was low and his manner modest—a great man who in the game of human affairs played below the limit of his abilities. McGlenn roused himself. When emphatic, he had a way of turning out his thumb and slowly hammering his knee with his fist. In his sky there was a cloud of pessimism, but the brightness of his speech threw a rainbow across it. He was a poet in the garb of a Diogenes. Many of his theories were wrong, but all were striking. Sometimes his sentences flashed like a scythe swinging in the sunshine.

Henry talked as he had never found occasion to talk before. These men inspired him, and in acknowledgment of this he said: "We may for years carry in our minds a sort of mist that we cannot shape into an idea. Suddenly we meet a man, and he speaks the word of life unto that mist, and instantly it becomes a thought."

Other members joined the group, and the conversation broke and flew into sharp fragments. McGlenn and Richmond began to wrangle.

"Your children may not read my books," said McGlenn, replying to some assertion that Richmond had made, "but your great-grandchildren will."

"Oh, that's possible," Richmond rejoined. "I can defend my immediate offspring, while my descendants may be left without protection. If you would tear the didacticism out of your books and inject a little more of the juice of human interest—hold on!" Richmond threw up his arm, as though warding off a blow. "When that double line comes between his eyes I always feel that he is going to hit me."

"I wouldn't hit you. I have some pity left."

"Or fear—which is it?"

"Not fear; pity."

"Why don't you reserve some of it for your readers?"

McGlenn frowned. "I don't expect you to like my books."

"Oh, you have realized the fact that the characters are wooden?"

"No, but I have realized that they are beyond your feeble grasp. I don't want you to like my books." He hammered his knee. "The book that wins your regard is an exceedingly bad production. When you search for facts you may sometimes go to high sources, but when you read fiction you go to the dogs. A consistent character in fiction is beyond you."

"There are no consistent characters in life," said Richmond, "and a consistent character in fiction is merely a strained form of art. In life the most arrant coward will sometimes fight; the bravest man at times lacks nerve; the generous man may sometimes show the spirit of the niggard. But your character in fiction is different. He must be always brave, or always generous, or always niggardly. He must be consistent, and consistency is not life."

"But inconsistency is life, and you are, therefore, not dead," McGlenn replied. "If inconsistency were a jewel," he added, "you would be a cluster of brilliants. As it is, you are an intellectual fault-finder and a physical hypochondriac."

"And you are an intellectual cartoon and a physical mistake."

"I won't talk to you. Even the semblance of a gentleman commands my respect, but I can't respect you. I like truth, but"—

"Is that the reason you seek me?"

"No, it is the reason I avoid you. Brutal prejudice never held a truth."

"Not when it shook hands with you," Richmond replied.

McGlenn got up, walked over to the piano, came back, looked at his watch, and addressing Richmond, asked:

"Are you going home, John?"

"Yes, John. Suppose we walk."

"I'll go you; come on."

They bade Henry good evening and together walked off affectionately.

"What do you think of our new friend?" Richmond asked as they strolled along.

"John, he has suffered. He is a great man."

"I don't know how he may turn out," Richmond said, "but I rather like him. Of course he hasn't fitted himself to his position—that is, he doesn't as yet feel the force of old Witherspoon's money. His experience has gone far toward making a man of him, but his changed condition may after a while throw his past struggles into contempt and thereby corrode his manliness."

"I don't think that he scraped up his principles from the Witherspoon side of the house," McGlenn declared. "If he had, we should at once have discovered in him the unmistakable trace of the hog. Oh, I don't think he will stay in the club very long. His tendency will be to drift away. All rich men are the enemies of democracy. If they pretend that they are not, they are hypocrites; if they believe they are not, it is because they haven't come to a correct understanding of themselves. The meanest difference that can exist between

Opie Read

men is the difference that money makes. There is some compassion in an intellectual difference, and even in a difference of birth there is some little atonement to be expected, but a moneyed difference is stiff with unyielding brutality."

In this opinion they struck a sort of agreement, but they soon fell apart, and they wrangled until they reached a place where their pathway split. They halted for a moment; they had been fierce in argument. Now they were calm.

"Can't you come over to-night, John?" McGlenn asked.

"No, I can't possibly come to-night, John. I've got a piece of work on hand and must get it off. I've neglected it too long already."

But he did go over that night, and he wrangled with McGlenn until twelve o'clock.

CHAPTER XIII

BUTTING AGAINST A WALL

When we have become familiar with an environment we sometimes wonder why at any time it should have appeared strange to us; and it was thus with Henry as the months moved along. The mansion in Prairie Avenue was now home-like to him, and the contrasts which its luxurious belongings were wont to summon were now less sharp and were dismissed with a growing easiness. Feeling the force which position urges, he worked without worry, and conscious of a certain ability, he did not question the success of his plans. But how much of the future did he intend these plans to cover? He turned from this troublesome uncertainty and found satisfaction in that state of mind which permits one day to forecast the day which is to follow, and on a futurity stretching further than this he resolutely turned his back. In his work and in his rest at the Press Club, whither he went every afternoon, he found his keenest pleasure. He was also fond of the theater, not to sit with a box party, but to loiter with Richmond—to enjoy the natural, to growl at the tame, and to leave the place whenever a tiresome dialogue came on. Ellen sometimes drew him into society, and on Sundays he usually went with Mrs. Witherspoon to a Congregational church where a preacher who had taught his countenance the artifice of a severe solemnity denounced the money-chasing spirit of the age at about double the price that he had received in the East.

The Witherspoons had much company and they entertained generously, though not with a showy lavishness, for the old man had a quick eye for the appearance of waste. It was noticeable, too, that since Henry came young women who were counted as Ellen's friends were more frequent with their visits. Witherspoon rarely laughed at anything, but he laughed at this. His wife, however, discovered in it no cause for mirth. A mother may plan the marriage of her daughter, for that is romantic, but she looks with an anxious eye upon the marriage of her son, for that is serious.

One evening, when Witherspoon and Henry had gone into the library to smoke, the merchant remarked: "I want, to talk to you about the course of your paper."

"All right, sir."

The merchant stood on the hearth-rug. He lighted his cigar, turned it round and round, and then said:

"Brooks called my attention this afternoon to an article on working girls. Does it meet with your approval?"

"Why, yes. It was a special assignment, and I gave it out."

"Hum!" Witherspoon grunted. He sat down in his leather-covered chair, crossed his legs, struck a match on the sole of his slipper, relighted his cigar, which he had suffered to go out, and for a time smoked in silence.

"Is there anything wrong about it?" Henry asked.

"I might ask you if there is anything right about it,"

Witherspoon replied. "'The poor ye have with you always,' was uttered by the Son of God. It was not only a prophecy, but a truth for all ages. There are grades in life, and who made them? Man. Ah, but who made man? God. Then who is responsible for the grades? Nature sets the example of inequality. One tree is higher than another." His cigar had gone out. He lighted it again and continued: "Writers who seek to benefit the poor of ten injure them—teach them a dissatisfaction which in its tarn brings a sort of reprisal on the part of capital."

"I don't agree with you," said Henry.

"Of course not."

"I have cause to know that you are wrong, sir."

"You think you have," the merchant replied.

"It is true," Henry admitted, "that we shall always have the poor with us."

"I thought so," said Witherspoon.

"But it is not true that an attempt to aid them is harmful. Their condition has steadily improved since history "—

"You are a sentimentalist."

"I am more than that," said Henry. "I am a man."

"Hum! And are you more than that?"

"How could I be more?"

"Easily enough. You could be an anarchist."

"And is that a step higher?"

"Wolves think so."

"But I don't"

"I hope not."

They sat in silence. The young man was angry, but he controlled himself.

"It is easy to scatter dangerous words in this town," said the merchant. "And, sir,"—he broke off, rousing himself,—"look at the inconsistency, the ridiculousness of your position. I employ more than a thousand people; my son says that I oppress them. I"—

"Hold on; I didn't say that. I don't know of any injustice that you inflict upon your employes; but I do know of such wrongs committed by other men. But you have shown me that the condition of those creatures is hopeless."

"What creatures?"

"Women who work for a living."

"And do you know the cause of their hopelessness?"

"Yes; poverty and oppression."

"Ah, but what is the cause of their poverty?"

"The greed of man."

"Oh, no; the appetite of man—whisky. Nine out of ten of those so-called wretched creatures can trace their wretchedness to drink."

"But it is not their fault."

"Oh!"

Henry was stunned. He saw what a wall he was butting against. "And is this to go on forever?" he asked.

"Yes, forever. 'The poor ye have with you always.'"

"But present conditions may be overturned."

"Possibly, but other conditions just as bad, or even worse, will build on the ruins. That is the history you spoke of just now."

"But slavery was swept away—and, let me affirm," he suddenly broke off, "that the condition of the poorer people in this town is worse than the slavery that existed in the South. From that slavery the government pointed toward freedom, and mill-owners in the North applauded—men, too, mind you, who were the hardest of masters. I can bring up now the picture of a green lane. I can see an old negro woman sweeping the door-yard of her cabin, and she sings a song. Her husband is at work in the field, and her happy children are fishing in the bayou. That is the freedom which the government pointed out—the freedom which a God-inspired Lincoln proclaimed. But do you hear any glad songs among the slaves in the North? Let me tell you, sir, that we are confronted with a problem that is more serious than that which was solved by Lincoln."

Witherspoon looked at him as though he could think of no reply. At one moment he seemed to be filling up with the gathering impulses of anger; at another he appeared to be humiliated.

"Are you my son?" he asked.

"Presumably. An impostor would yield to your demands; he would win your confidence that he might steal your money."

"Yes," said the merchant, and he sat in silence.

Henry was the first to speak. "If you were poor, and with the same intelligence you have now, what would you advise the poor man to do?"

"I should advise him to do as I did when I was poor and as I do now—work. Now, let me tell you something: Last year your mother and I gave away a great deal of money—we do so every year. Does that look as if I am grinding the poor? You have hurt me."

"I am sorry. But if I have hurt you with a truth, it should make you think."

Witherspoon looked at him, and this time it was with resentment. "What! you talk about making me think? Young man, you don't know what it is to think. You are confounded with the difference between sentimentalism and thought. You go ahead and print your newspaper and don't worry about the workingwoman. Her class will be larger and worse off, probably, a hundred years after you are dead."

"Yes, but before that time her class may rise up and sweep everything before it. A democracy can't long permit a few men to hold all the wealth. But there's no good to come from a discussion with you."

"You are right," said Witherspoon, "but hold on a moment.

Don't go away believing that I have no sympathy for the poor. I have, but I haven't time to worry with it. There is no reason why any man should be poor in this country."

Henry thought of a hundred things to say, but said nothing. He knew that it was useless; he knew that this man's strength had blinded him to the weakness of other men, and he felt that American aristocracy was the most grinding of all aristocracies, for the reason that a man's failure to reach its grade was attributable to himself alone.

CHAPTER XIV

A DIFFERENT HANDWRITING

Henry bade Witherspoon good night and went to his room. A fire was burning in the grate. At the window there was a rattle of sleet. He lighted his old briar-root pipe and sat down. He had, as usual, ceased to argue with himself; he simply mused. He acknowledged his weakness, and sought a counteracting strength, but found none. But why should he fight against good fortune? It was not his fault that certain conditions existed. Why not starve the past and feed the present? But he had begun to argue, and he shook himself as though he would be freed from something that had taken hold of him, and he got up and stood at the window. How raw the night! And as he stood there, he fancied that the darkness and the sleet of his boyhood were trying to force their way into the warmth and the light of his new inheritance. He turned suddenly about, and bowing with mock politeness, said to himself: "You are a fool." He lighted his pipe afresh, and sat down to work. Some one tapped at the door. Was it Witherspoon come to deliver another argument, and to decide again in his own favor? No, it was Ellen. She had been at the theater.

"You bring roses out of the storm," said Henry, in allusion to the color of her cheeks.

"But I don't bring flattery. Gracious! I am chilled through."
She took off her gloves and held her hands over the grate.
"Everybody's gone to bed, and I didn't know but you might
be here, scribbling. Goodness, what's that you've been
smoking?"

"A pipe."

She turned from the fire and shrugged her shoulders.
"Couldn't you get a cigar? Why do you smoke that awful
thing?"

"It is an altar of the past, and on it I burn the memories of its
day," he answered, smiling.

"Well, I think I would get a new altar and burn incense for
the present! Oh, but I've had the stupidest evening."

"Wasn't the play good?"

"No, it was talk, talk, with a stress laid on nothing. And then
my escort wasn't particularly entertaining."

"Who?"

"Oh, a Mr. Somebody. What have you been doing all the
evening?"

"Something that I found to be worse than useless. Father and
I have been locking horns over the—not exactly the labor
question, but over the wretchedness of working-women."

"What do you know about the wretchedness of working-
women?" she asked.

"What do I know about it? What can I help knowing about

it? How can I shut my eyes against it?"

"I don't see why they are so very wretched. They get pay, I'm sure. Somebody has to work; somebody has to be poor. What are you writing?"

"The necessary rot of an editorial page." he answered.

"Why, how your handwriting has changed," she said, leaning over the table.

"How so?"

"Why, this is so different from the letters you wrote before you came home."

He did not reply immediately; he was thinking. "Pens in that country cut queer capers," he said. "Where are those letters, anyway?"

"Mother has put them away somewhere."

"I should like to see them again."

"Why?"

"Oh, on account of the memories they hold. Get them for me, and I will give you a description of my surroundings at the time I wrote them."

"Why, what a funny fellow you are! Can't you give me a description anyway?"

"No, not a good one."

"But I don't want to wake mother, and I don't know that I can find the letters."

"Go and see."

"Oh, you are so headstrong."

She went out, and he walked up and down the room, and then stood again at the window. Ellen returned.

"Here they are."

"Did you wake mother?"

"No, but I committed burglary. I found the key and unlocked her trunk, and all to please you."

"Good, and for the first time burglary shall be repaid with gratitude."

He took the letters and looked at the sprawling characters drawn by the hand of his friend. "When I copied this confession," said he, "I was heavy of heart. I was sitting in a small room, looking far down into a valley where nature seemed to keep her darkness stored, and from, another window, in the east, I could see a mountain where she made her light."

"Go on," she said, leaning with her elbows on the table.

He began to walk across the room, from the door to the grate, and to talk as one delivering a set oration. "And I had just finished my work when a most annoying monkey, owned by the landlord, jumped through the window. I was so startled that I threw the folded papers at him"—

"What have you done!" she cried.

He had thrown the letters into the fire, he sprang forward, and snatching them, threw them on the hearth and stamped out the blaze.

"Oh, I do wish you hadn't done that," she said, hoarse with alarm. "Mother reads these letters every day, and—oh, I *do* wish you hadn't done it! They are all scorched—ruined, and I wouldn't have her know that I took them out of her trunk for anything. What shall we do about it? Oh, I know you didn't mean to do it." He had looked appealingly at her. "I wish I hadn't got them."

"It is only the copy of the confession that is badly burned. The original is here on the table," he said.

"I know, but what good will that do? The letters are so scorched that it won't do to return them."

"But I can copy them," he replied.

"Oh, you genius!" she exclaimed, clapping her hands.

"Thank you," he said, bowing. Then he added: "Let me see— this paper won't do. Where can we get some fool's-cap?"

"There must be some in the library," she answered. "I'll slip down and see."

She hastened down-stairs and soon returned with the paper. "I feel like a burglar," she said.

"And I *am* a forger," he replied.

"Won't take you long, will it?"

"No."

The work was soon completed. The scorched letters were thrown into the fire. "She will never know the difference," said Ellen. "It is a sin to deceive her, but then, following the burglary, deception is a kindness; and there can't be so very much wickedness in a sin that keeps one from being unhappy."

"Or keeps one from being discovered," he suggested. She laughed, not mirthfully, but with an attempt at self-consolation. "This is our first secret," she said, as she opened the door.

"And I think you will keep it," he replied, smiling at her.

She looked at him for a moment and rejoined: "Indeed, fellow-criminal! And if you didn't smoke that horrid pipe, what a lovable convict you would make."

When she was gone he stood again at the window. The night was breathing hard. He spoke to himself with mock concern: "Two hours ago you were simply a fool, but now you are a scoundrel."

CHAPTER XV

TOLD HIM HER STORY

When he awoke the next morning his blood seemed to be clogged somewhere far from the seat of thought, and then it came with a leap that brought back the night before. "But I won't argue with you," he said, turning over. "Argue," he repeated. "Why, it's past argument now. I will simply do the best I can and let the worst take care of itself. But I do despise a vacillator, and I am one. The old man maybe right. Nature admires strength and never pities the weak. And what am I to do if I'm not to carry out my part of this programme? The trial is over," he said as he got up. "I am Henry Witherspoon."

He was busy in his room at the office when Brooks entered.

"Well, hard at it, I see."

"Yes. Sit down; I'll be through with this in a moment."

He sat himself back from the desk, and Brooks asked, "Can't you go out to lunch with me?"

"Isn't time yet."

"Hardly, that's so," Brooks admitted, looking at his watch. "I happened to have business in this neighborhood and thought I'd drop in. Say," he added in a lower tone, and nodding his head toward the door of the adjoining room, "who is she?"

"The literary reviewer."

"She's a stunner. What's her name?"

"Miss Drury."

"You might introduce me."

"She's busy."

"Probably she'd go to lunch with us."

"She refuses to go out with any one."

"Hasn't been here long, eh?" That was the floorwalker's idea. "Well, I must get back, if you can't go with me. So long."

Henry took a book into Miss Drury's room. "Here's something that was sent to me personally," said he, "but treat it as you think it deserves."

She looked up with a suggestion of a smile. "Are you willing to trust the reputation of your friends to me?" she asked.

"I am at least willing to let you take charge of their vanity."

"Oh, am I so good a keeper of vanity?"

"No, you are so gentle an exterminator of it."

"Thank you," she said, laughing. Her hair seemed ready to

break from its fastenings, and she gave it those deft touches
of security which are mysterious to man, but which a little
girl practices on a doll.

"You have wonderful hair," he said.

And she answered: "I'm going to cut it off."

This is woman's almost invariable reply to such a compliment. Henry knew that she would say it, and she knew that
she would not cut it off, and they both laughed.

"How did you happen to get into newspaper work?" he
asked.

Her face became serious. "I had to do something," she
answered, "and I couldn't do anything else. My mother was
an invalid for ten years, and I nursed her, read to her day and
night. Sometimes in the winter she couldn't sleep, and I
would get up and amuse her by writing reviews of the books
I had read. It was only play, but after she was dead I thought
that I might make it earnest."

"And your father died when you were very young, I
suppose."

She looked away, and with both hands she began to touch
her hair again. "Yes," she said.

"Tell me about him."

"Why about him?"

"I don't know. Because you have told me about your mother,
I suppose."

"And are you so much interested in me?" she asked, looking earnestly at him.

"Yes."

"I ought not to tell you, but I will. We lived in the country. My father was"—She looked about her and then at him. "My father was a drunkard, but my mother loved him devotedly. One day he went to the village, several miles away, and at evening he didn't come home, and my mother knew the cause. It was a cold, snowy night. Mother stood at the gate, holding a lantern. She wouldn't let me stand there with her, it was so cold, but I was on my knees in a chair at the window, and I could see her. She stood there so long, and it seemed so cruel that I should be in a warm room while she was out in the cold, that I slipped out and closed the door softly after me. I stood a short distance behind her, and I had not been standing there long when a horse, covered with snow, came stumbling out of the darkness. Mother called me, and I ran to her. We went down the road, holding the lantern first one side, then the other, that we might see into the corners of the fences. We found him lying dead in the road, covered with snow. Mother was never well after that night—but really I am neglecting my work."

He returned to his desk. The proof-sheets of a leading article were brought to him, but he sat gazing at naught that he could see.

"Are you done with those proofs?" some one asked.

"Take them away," he said, without looking up. He sat for a long time, musing, and then he shook himself, a habit which he had lately formed in trying to free himself from meditations that sought to possess him.

He went out to luncheon, and just as he was going into a restaurant some one spoke to him. It was old man Colton.

"My dear Mr. Witherspoon," said the old man, "come and have a bite to eat with me. Ah, come on, now; no excuse. Let's go this way. I know of a place that will just suit you. This way. I'm no hand for clubs—they bore me; they are newfangled."

The old man conducted him into a basement restaurant not noticeable for cleanliness, but strong with a smell of mutton.

"Now, suppose we try a little broth," said the old man, when they had sat down. "Two bowls of mutton broth," he added, speaking to the waiter. "Ah," he went on, "you may talk about your dishes, but at noontime there is nothing that can touch broth. And besides," he added, in a whisper, "there's no robbery in broth. These restaurant fellows are skinners of the worst order. I'll tell you, my dear Mr. Witherspoon, everything teaches us to practice economy. We must do it; it's the saving clause of life. Now, what could be better than this? Go back to work, and your head's clear. My dear Mr. Witherspoon, if I had been a spendthrift, I should not only be a pauper—I should have been dead long ago."

He continued to talk on the virtues of economy. "Won't you have some more broth?"

"No, thank you."

"Won't you have something else?" he asked, in a tone that implied extreme fear.

"No, I'm not hungry to-day."

This announcement appeared greatly to relieve the old man.

"Oh, you'll succeed in life, my dear young man; but really you ought to come into the store with us. It would do your father so much good; he would feel that he has a sure hold on the future, you understand. You don't know what a comfort Brooks is to me. Why, if my daughter had married a man in any other line, I—well, it would have been a great disappointment. Are you going back to work now?"

"No; to the Press Club."

"Why don't you come to see us oftener?"

"Oh, I'm there often enough, I should think—two or three times a week."

"Yes, of course, but we are all so anxious that you should become interested in our work. Don't discourage yourself with the belief that a man brought up in the South is not a good business man. I am from the South, my dear Mr. Witherspoon."

They had reached the sidewalk, and the roar from the street impelled the old man to force his squeaky voice into a split shout.

"Southern man"—He was bumped off by the passing throng, but he got back again and shouted: "Southern man has just as good commercial ability as anybody. Well, I must leave you here."

CHAPTER XVI

AN AROUSER OF THE SLEEPY

In the Press Club Henry found Mr. Flummers haranguing a party of men who sat about the round table. He stood that he might have room in which to scallop his gestures, and he had reached a climax just as Henry joined the circle. He waited until all interruptions had ceased and then continued: "Milwaukee was asleep, and I was sent up there to arouse it. But I shook it too hard; I hadn't correctly measured my own strength. The old-timers said, 'Let us doze,' but I commanded, 'Wake up here now, and get a move on you,' and they had to wake up. But they formulated a conspiracy against me, and I was removed."

"How were you removed, Mr. Flummers?" McGlenn asked.

"Oh, a petition, signed by a thousand sleepy citizens, was sent down here to my managing editor, and I was requested to come away. Thus was my Milwaukee career ended, but it ended in a blaze that dazzled the eyes of the old-timers." He cut a scallop. "But papa was not long idle. The solid South wanted him. They knew that papa was the man to quiet a disturbance or compel a drowsy municipality to get up and rub its eyes. Well, I went to Memphis. What was the cause of the great excitement that followed?" He tapped his forehead.

"Papa's nut. But again had he underestimated himself; again was he too strong for the occasion. He tossed up the community in his little blanket, and while it was still in the air, papa skipped, and the railroad train didn't go any too fast for him."

"And was that the time you went over into Arkansas and murdered a man?" Richmond asked.

"Oh, no; you are mixing ancient history with recent events. But say, John, you haven't bought anything to-day."

"Why, you paunch-bulging liar, I bought you a drink not more than ten minutes ago."

"But you owed me that one."

"Get out, you nerveless beef! Under the old law for debt I could put you in prison for life."

"Oh, no."

"Do you really need a drink, Mr. Flummers?" McGlenn asked.

"Yes."

"And you don't think that there is any mistake about it?"

"No."

"Well, then, as one who has been compelled to love you, I will buy you a drink."

"Good stuff. Say, Whit, touch the bell over there, will you?"

"Touch it yourself, you lout!"

With a profane avowal that he had never struck so lazy a party, Flummers rang the bell, and when the boy appeared, he called with hearty hospitality: "See what the gentlemen will have."

"Would you like something more?" Henry asked of Flummers, when the drinks had been served.

"Oh, I've just had one. But wait a minute. Say, boy, bring me a cigar."

When the cigar was brought, Flummers said, "That's the stuff!" and a moment later he broke out with, "Say, Witherspoon, why don't you kill the geyser that does the county building for your paper?"

"Why so?"

"Oh, he flashes his star and calls himself a journalist. What time is it? I must hustle; can't stay here and throw away time on you fellows. Say, John"—

Richmond shut him off with: "Don't call me John. A man— I'll say man out of courtesy to your outward form—a man that hasn't sense enough to lift a bass into a boat is not to be permitted such a familiarity. Out in a boat with him last summer and caught a big bass," Richmond explained to the company, "and brought it up to the side of the boat and told Flummers to lift it in, not thinking at the time that he hadn't sense enough, and he grabbed hold of the line and let the fish get away. It made me sick, and I had a strong fight with myself to keep from drowning him."

Flummers tapped his forehead. "Papa's nut says, 'Keep your

hand out of a fish's mouth.' Oh, I don't want to go fishing with you again. No fun for me to pull a boat and see a man thrash the water. Say, did I take anything on you just now?" he suddenly broke off, addressing Henry.

"Yes, but you can have something else."

"Well, not now. I'll hold it in reserve. In this life it is well to have reserve forces stationed here and there. Who's got a car-ticket? I've got to go over on the West Side. What, are you all broke? What sort of a poverty-stricken gang have I struck? Well, I've given you as much of my valuable time as I can spare."

"I suppose you are getting used to this town," said Mortimer, when Flummers was gone.

"Yes, I am gradually making myself feel at home," Henry answered.

"You find the weather disagreeable, of course. We do, I know."

"I think that Chicago is great in spite of its climate," said Henry.

"If great at all, it is great in spite of a great many absences," McGlenn replied; "and in these absences it is mean and contemptible. To money it gives worship; to the song and dance man it pays admiring attention, but to the writer it gives neglect—the campaign of silence."

Richmond put his hand to his month and threw his head back. "The trouble with you, John"—

"There's no trouble with me."

"Yes, there is, and it is the trouble that comes to all men who form an estimate without having first taken the trouble to think."

"Gentlemen," said McGlenn, "I wish to call your attention to that remark. John Richmond advising people to think before they form their estimates. John, you are the last man to think before you form an estimate. Within a minute after you meet a man you are prepared to give your estimate of his character; you'll give a half-hour's opinion on a minute's acquaintance."

"Some people can't form an opinion of a man after a year's acquaintance with him, but I can. I go by a certain instinct, and when the wrong sort of man rubs up against me I know it. I don't need to wait until he has worked me before I find out that he is an impostor. But, as I was going to say, the trouble with you is that you forget the difference that exists between new and old cities. A new community worships material things; and if it pays tribute to an idea, it must be that idea which appeals quickest to the eye—to the commoner senses. And in this Chicago is no worse than other raw cities. Fifty years from now "—

"Who wants to live fifty years in this miserable world?" McGlenn broke in. "There is but one community in which the writer is at ease, and that is the community of death. It is populous; it is crowded with writers, but it holds an easy place for every one. The silence of that community frightens the rich but its democracy pleases the poor."

"I suppose, then, that you want to die."

"I do."

"But you didn't want to die yesterday?"

"Yes, it was the very time when I should have died—I had just eaten a good dinner. You don't know how to eat, John. You stuff yourself, John. Yes, you stuff yourself and think that you have dined. The reason is that you have never taken the trouble to become civilized. It's my misfortune to have friends who can't eat. But some of my friends can eat, and they are therefore great men. Tod Cowles strikes a new dish at a house on the North Side and softens his voice and says, 'Ah hah.' He is a great man, for he knows that he has discovered an additional pleasure to offset another trouble of this infamous life; and Colonel Norton is a great man—he knows how to eat; but you, John, are an outcast from the table, and therefore civilization cannot reach you. Civilization comes to the feast and asks, 'Where is John Richmond, whom I heard some of you say something about?' and we reply, 'He holds us in contempt,' and Civilization pronounces these solemn words: 'He who holds ye in contempt, the same will I banish.'"

"But," rejoined Richmond, "civilization teaches one of two things—to think or to become a glutton. Somehow I was kept away from the feast and had to accept the other teaching. I don't go about deifying my stomach and making an apostle of the palate of my month. When I eat"—

"But you don't eat; you stuff. I have sat down to a table with you, and after giving your order you would fill yourself so full of bread and pickles or anything within reach that you couldn't eat anything when the order was brought."

"That was abstraction of thought instead of hunger," Richmond replied.

"No, it was the presence of gluttony. Can you eat, Mr. Witherspoon?"

"I fear that I must confess a lack of higher civilization. I am not well schooled in anything, and I suppose that you must class me with Richmond—as a barbarian. I lack"—

"Art," McGlenn suggested. "But for you there is a chance. John Richmond is hopelessly gone."

"I sometimes feed my dogs on stewed tripe," said Whittlesy, "and the good that it does them teaches me that man is to be judged largely by what he eats."

"There is absolutely no use for all this bloody rot," Mortimer declared. "Eating is essential, of course, but I don't see how men can talk for an hour on the subject, and talk foolishly, at that."

"If eating is essential," Richmond replied, "it is a wonder that you don't kick against it."

"Ah, but isn't it a good thing that I don't kick against non-essentials? Wouldn't I be obliged to kick against this assemblage and its beastly rot?"

Mortimer sometimes emphasized his walk with a peculiar springiness of step, and with this emphasis he walked off, biting the stem of his pipe.

"I thought that by this time you would begin to show a weariness of the Press Club," McGlenn said to Henry.

"I don't see why you should have thought that. I said at first that I was one of you."

"Yes, but I didn't know but by this time you might have discovered your mistake."

"I made no mistake, and therefore could discover none. Let me tell you that between George Witherspoon's class and me there is but little affinity. You may call me a crank, and perhaps I am, but I was poor so long that I felt a sort of pride in the fight I was compelled to make. Poverty has its arrogance, and foppery is sometimes found in rags. I don't mind telling you that I have been strongly urged to take what is called my place in the world; but that place is so distasteful to me that I look on it with a shudder. I despise barter—I am compelled to buy, but I am not forced to sell. I am not a sentimentalist—if I were I should attempt to write poetry. I am not a philosopher—if I were I shouldn't attempt to run a newspaper. I am simply an ordinary man who has passed through an extraordinary school. And what I think are virtues may be errors."

McGlenn replied: "John is your friend. John thinks that you are a strong man—I don't know yet, but I do know that you please me when you are silent and that you don't displease me when you talk. You are strong enough to say, 'I don't know,' and a confession of ignorance is a step toward wisdom. Ask John a question to-day and he may say, 'I don't know,' but to-morrow he does know—he has spent a night with it. You are a remarkable man, Mr. Witherspoon," he added after a moment's reflection, "a very remarkable man. Your life up to a short time ago, you say, was a struggle; your uncle was a poor man. Suddenly you became the son of a millionaire. A weak nature would straightway have assumed the airs of a rich man; you remained a democrat. It was so remarkable that I thought the decision might react as an error, and therefore I asked if you had not begun to grow weary of this democracy, the Press Club."

McGlenn smiled, and his smile had two meanings, one for his friends and another for his enemies. His friends saw a thoughtful countenance illumined by an intellectual light; his enemies recognized a sarcasm that had escaped from a sly and revengeful spirit. But Henry was his friend.

"John," said Richmond, "you think"—

McGlenn turned out his thumb and began to motion with his fist. "I won't submit to the narrow dictum of a man who presumes to tell me what I think."

"But if nobody were to tell you, how would you find out what you think? Oh," he added, "I admit that it was presumption on my part. I was presuming that you think."

"I do think, and if some one must tell me *what* I think, let him be a thinking man."

"John, you cry out for thought, and are the first to strike at it with your dogmatism. You don't think—you dogmatize."

McGlenn turned to Henry. "I had two delightful days last week. John Richmond was out of town."

"Yes," said Richmond, putting his feet on a chair. "Falsehood gallops in riotous pleasure when Truth is absent. Hold on! I can stand one wrinkle between your eyes, but I am afraid of two."

"A man of many accomplishments, but wholly lacking in humor," said McGlenn, seeming to study Richmond for the purpose of placing an appraisement on him. "A man who worships Ouida and decries Sir Richard Steele."

"No, I don't worship Ouida, but I read her sometimes because she is interesting. As for Steele, he is decried by your praise. Say, John, you advised me to change grocers every month, and I don't know but it would be a good plan.

An old fellow that I have been trading with has sent me a bill for eighty-three dollars."

"John, he probably takes you for a great man and wants to compliment you."

"I don't object to a compliment, but that was flattery," Richmond, replied, taking his feet off one chair and putting them on another. "Let's ride home, John; it's 'most too slippery to walk."

"All right. You have ruined my health already by making me walk with you. Come on; we'll go now."

CHAPTER XVII

AN OLD MAN WOULD INVEST

When Henry went home to dinner he found, already seated at the table, old man Colton, Mrs. Colton and Mrs. Brooks. The old Marylander got away from his soup, got off his chair, and greeted Henry with an effusive display of what might have been his pleasure at seeing the young man, but which had more of the appearance of a palavering pretense. He bowed, ducked his head first on one side and then on the other—and his colored handkerchief dangled at his coat-tails. He found his tongue, which at first he seemed to have lost, and with his bald head bobbing about, he appeared as an aged child, prattling at random.

"Hah, hah, delighted to see you again, my dear young man. Didn't know that I was coming when you were so kind as to take lunch with me to-day; ladies came in the afternoon; Brooks couldn't come with me, but he will be here later on. Hah, hah, they are taking excellent care of us, you see. Ah, you sit here by me? Glad."

Mrs. Colton was exceedingly feeble, and her daughter appeared as a very old-fashioned girl in a stylish habit—an old daguerreotype sort of face, smooth, shiny and expressionless.

"We have all been talking about you," Colton said, as Henry sat down. "Your mother and sister think you a very wonderful man, and my dear friend Witherspoon"—

"Brother Colton is from Maryland," Witherspoon remarked.

Colton laughed and ducked his head. Ah, the listless wit of the rich! It may be pointless, but how laughable is the millionaire's joke.

"But, my dear young man, we are determined to have you with us," Colton declared, when he had recovered himself. He nodded at Witherspoon.

"We are going to try," the great merchant replied. "By the way, I told Brooks that we'd have to press Bradley & Adams, of Atchison, Kansas. They are altogether too slow—there's no excuse for it."

"None in the world; none whatever," Colton agreed. He more than agreed, for there was alarm in his voice, and the alarm of an old miser is pitiable. "Gracious alive, can they expect people to wait always? Dear, what can the world be coming to when we are all to be cheated out of our rights? We'll have the law on them."

Money professes great love for the law, and not without cause. The rich man thinks that the law is his; and the poor man says, "It was not made for me."

Among the ladies Henry was the subject of a subdued discussion, and occasionally he heard Mrs. Colton say: "Such a comfort to you, and after so many years of separation. So manly." And then Mrs. Brooks would say: "Yes, indeed."

Henry noticed that Colton was not accompanied with his mutton-broth economy. It was evident that the old man was frugal only to his own advantage, and that his heartiness came at the expense of other men.

Brooks arrived soon after dinner. The women went to the drawing-room to talk about Henry, and to exchange harmless hypocrisies, and the men betook themselves to the library to smoke and to discuss plots that are known as enterprises. Country merchants were taken up, turned over, examined and put down ruined. Brooks was as keen and as ardent as a prosecuting attorney. Every man who owed a bill was under indictment.

"You see," he said to Henry, "we have to hold these fellows tight or they would get loose and smash us."

"You needn't apologize to me," Henry replied.

"Of course not, but as you say that you don't understand business, I merely wanted to show you to what extent we are driven."

"Oh, I assure you that it is awfully unpleasant," said Colton, "but we have to do it. And let me tell you, my dear young man, there is more crime than you imagine in the neglect of these fellows. In this blessed country there is hardly any excuse for a man's failure to meet his obligations. The trouble is that people who can't afford it live too high. Let them economize; let them be sensible. Why, I could have gone broke forty-odd years ago; hah, I could go broke now. Oh, I know that we are all accused of being hard, but you have no idea what the wealthy people of this city do for the poor. Just look at the charity balls; look at our annual showing, and you'll find it remarkable."

Henry felt that the charity of the rich was largely a species of "bluff" that they make at one another. It was not real charity; it was an advertisement—it was business.

"My dear friend Witherspoon," said Colton, mouthing his cigar—he did not smoke at home—"I am going to branch out more. I'm going to make investments. I see that it is safe, and I want you to help me."

"All right; how much do you want to invest?"

"Oh, I can place my hand on a little money—just a little. I've got some in stocks, but I've got a little by me."

"How much?"

This frightened him. "Oh, I don't know; really, I can't tell. But I think that I've got a little that I'd like to invest. But I'll talk to you about it to-morrow."

"All right."

"I think real estate would be about the right thing. I could soon turn it over, you know. Some wonderfully fortunate investments have been made that way. But I'll talk to you about it to-morrow."

Brooke said that he was in something of a hurry to get home, and the visitors took their leave early in the evening. Witherspoon returned to the library after going to the door with Colton. He sat down, stretched forth his feet, meditated for a few moments, and said: "The bark on a beech tree was never any closer than that old man, and yet he is kind-hearted."

"When kindness doesn't cost anything, I suppose," Henry suggested.

"Yes, that's true. He spoke of the wonderful showing of the charities of this city as though he were a prime mover in them, when, in fact, I don't think he ever contributed more than a barrel of flour in any one year. But he is a good business man, and if there were more like him there would be fewer bankrupts."

Ellen appeared at the door. "Henry, mother and I are going to your room to pay you a call."

"All right, I'll go up with you. Won't you come, father?"

"No, I believe not. Think I'll read a while and go to bed."

Henry's room was bright with a gladsome fire. On the table had been set a vase of moss roses, and beside the vase lay an old black pipe, tied with a blue ribbon. The young man laughed, and the girl said:

"Mother's doings. Ugh! the nasty thing!"

"If my son smoked a pipe when he was in exile," Mrs. Witherspoon replied, "he can do so now. None of the privileges of a strange land shall be denied him in his own home."

She sat in an easy-chair and was slowly rocking. To man a rocking-chair is a remembrancer of a mother's affection.

"Light your pipe, my son."

"No, not now, mother."

Ellen sat on an arm of Henry's chair. "Your hair would curl if you were to encourage it," she remarked.

"Has anybody said anything about curly hair?" he asked.

"No, but I was just thinking that yours might curl."

"Do you want me to look like Brooks?"

She frowned. "He kinks his with a hot poker. I don't like pretty men."

"How about handsome men?"

"Oh, I have to like them. You are a handsome man, you know."

"Nonsense," he replied.

"Your grandmother was a very handsome woman," said Mrs. Witherspoon. "She had jet-black hair, and her teeth were like pearls. Ellen, what did Mr. Coglin say when you gave him the slippers?" Mr. Coglin was a clergyman.

"Oh, he thanked me, of course. He couldn't very well have said, 'Take them away.'"

"But did you tell him that you embroidered them with your own hands?"

"Yes, I told him."

"Then what did he say?"

"He pretended to be greatly surprised, and said something, but I have forgotten what it was. Mrs. Brooks is awful tiresome with her 'Yes, indeed,' isn't she? Seems to me that I'd learn something else."

"She's hardly so tiresome with her 'Yes, indeed,' as her father is with his 'Hah, hah, my dear Mr. Witherspoon,'" Henry replied.

"But he is a very old man, my son," said Mrs. Witherspoon, "and you must excuse him. I have heard that he was quite aristocratic before the war."

"Oh, he never was aristocratic," Ellen declared. "Aristocracy hampered by extreme stinginess would cut but a poor figure, I should think."

"Have we set up a grill here?" Henry asked.

Mrs. Witherspoon nodded at Ellen as if to emphasize the rebuke, and the young woman exclaimed: "Oh, I'm singled out, am I? Who said that the old man's 'hah, hah,' was tiresome? You'd better nod at your son, mother."

But she gave her son never a nod. In her sight he surely could commit no indiscretion. A moment later the mother asked:

"Have they talked to you again about going into the store?"

"Oh, they hint at it occasionally."

"Ellen, can't you find a chair? I know your brother must he tired." Ellen got off the arm of Henry's chair, and soon afterward Mrs. Witherspoon took the vacated place. The young woman laughed, but said nothing. The mother fondly touched Henry's hair and smoothed it back from his forehead. "Don't you let them worry you, my son. They can't help but respect your manliness. Indeed," she added, growing strangely bold for one so gentle, "must a man be a merchant whether he will or not? And whenever you want to write about poor women, you do it. They are mistreated; they are made wretched, and by just such men as Brooks, too. What does he care for a woman's misery? And your father's so blind that he doesn't see it. But I see it. And I oughtn't to say it, but I will—he has the impudence to tell your father that I give too much money to the poor. It's none of his business, I'm sure."

There was a peculiar softness in Henry's voice when he replied: "I hope some time to catch him interfering with your affairs."

"Oh, but you mustn't say a word, my son—not a word; and I don't want your father to know that I have said anything."

"He shall not know, but I hope some time to catch Brooks interfering with your affairs. He has meddled with mine, but I can forgive that."

Henry walked up and down the room when Mrs. Witherspoon and Ellen were gone. With a mother's love, that gentle woman had found a mother's place in his heart. He looked at the rocking-chair. Suddenly he seized hold of the mantelpiece to steady himself. He had caught himself seriously wondering if she had rocked him years ago.

CHAPTER XVIII

THE INVESTMENT

It seemed to Henry that he had just dozed off to sleep when he was startled by a loud knock at the door.

"Henry, Henry!" It was Witherspoon's voice.

"Yes."

"Get up, quick! Old man Colton is murdered."

When he went down-stairs he found the household in confusion. Every one on the place had been aroused. The servants were whispering in the hall. Witherspoon was waiting for him.

"A messenger has just brought the news. Come, we must go over there. The carriage is waiting."

It was two o'clock. A fierce and cutting wind swept across the lake—the icy breath of a dying year. Not a word was spoken as the carriage sped along. At the door of Colton's home Witherspoon and Henry were confronted by a policeman.

"My orders are to let no one in," said the officer.

"I am George Witherspoon."

The policeman stepped aside. Brooks met them in the hall. He said nothing, but took Witherspoon's hand. The place was thronged with police officers and reporters.

Adjoining Colton's sleeping-apartment, on the second floor, was a small room with a window looking out on the back yard, and with one door opening from the hall. In this room, let partly into the wall, was an iron safe in which the old man kept "the little money" that he had decided to invest in real estate. The window was protected by upright iron bars. At night, a gas-jet, turned low, threw dismal shadows about the room, and it was the old man's habit to light the gas at bed-time and to turn it off the first thing at morning. He had lighted the gas shortly after returning from Witherspoon's house and had gone to bed, and it must have been about one o'clock when the household was startled by the report of a pistol. Brooks and his wife, whose room was on the same floor, ran into the old man's room. The place was dark, but a bright light burned in the vault-room. Into this room they ran, and there, lying on the floor, with money scattered about him, was the old man, bloody and dead, with a bullet-hole in his breast. But where was Mrs. Colton? They hastened back to her room and struck a light. The old woman lay across the bed, unable to move—paralyzed.

The first discovery made by the police was that the iron bars at the window, four in number, had been sawed in two; and then followed another discovery of a more singular nature. In the window, caught by the sudden fall of the sash, was a black frock coat. In one of the tail pockets was a briar-root pipe. The sash had fallen while the murderer was getting out, and, pulled against the sash, the pipe held the garment fast.

One sleeve was torn nearly off. In a side pocket was found a letter addressed to Dave Kittymunks, general delivery, Chicago, and post-marked Milwaukee. Under the window a ladder was found.

At the coroner's inquest, held the next day, one of the servants testified that three days before, while the old man and Brooks were at the store and while the ladies were out, a man with black whiskers, and who wore a black coat, had called at the house and said that he had been sent to search for sewer-gas. He had an order presumably signed by Mr. Colton, and was accordingly shown through the house. He had insisted upon going into the vault-room, declaring that he had located the gas there, but was told that the room was always kept locked. He then went away. The servant had not thought to tell Mr. Colton.

A general delivery clerk at the post-office testified that the letter addressed to Dave Kittymunks had passed through his hands. The oddness of the name had fastened it on his memory. He did not think that he could identify the man who had received the letter, but he recalled the black whiskers. The letter was apparently written by a woman, and was signed "Lil." It was an urgent appeal for money.

CHAPTER XIX

ARRESTED EVERYWHERE

"Who is Dave Kittymunks?" was a question asked by the newspapers throughout the country. Not the slightest trace of him could be found, nor could "Lil" be discovered with any degree of certainty. But one morning the public was fed to an increase of appetite by an article that appeared in a Chicago newspaper. "Kittymunks came to Chicago about five months ago," said the writer, "and for a time went under the name of John Pruett. Fierce in his manner, threatening in his talk, wearing a scowl, frowning at prattling children and muttering at honest men, he repelled every one. Dissatisfied with his lot in life, he refused, even for commensurate compensation, to perform that honest labor which is the province of every true man, and like a hyena, he prowled about growling at himself and despising fate. The writer met him on several occasions and held out inducements that might lead to conversation, but was persistently repulsed by him. He frowned upon society, and set the grinding heel of his disapproval on every attempt to draw him out. Was there some dark mystery connected with his life? This question the writer asked himself. He execrated humanity; and, moody and alone, the writer has seen him sitting on a bench on the lake front, turning with a sullen look and viewing with suppressed rage the architectural grandeur towering at his back."

The article was written by Mr. Flummers. As the only reporter who could write from contact with the murderer, his sentences were bloated into strong significance. Fame reached down and snatched him up, and the blue light of his flambeau played about him.

"Pessimist as he is"—Flummers was holding forth among the night reporters at the central station—"Pessimist as he is, and a skeptic though he may be, papa goes through this life with his eyes open. Idle suggestion says, 'Shut your eyes, papa, and be happy,' but shrewdness says, 'Watch that fellow going along there.' I don't claim any particular credit for this; we are not to be vain of what nature has done for us, nor censured for what she has denied. We are all children, toddling about as an experiment, and wondering what we are going to be. Some of us fall and weep over our bruises, and some of us—some of us get there. He, he, he."

"Flummers, have they raised your salary yet?" some one asked.

"Oh, no, and that's why I am disgusted with the newspaper profession. The country cries out, 'Who is the man?' There is a deep silence. The country cries again, 'Does any one know this man?' And then papa speaks. But what does he get? The razzle. A great scoop rewarded with a razzle. My achievements are taken too much us a matter of course. I don't assert myself enough. I am too modest. Say, I smell liquor. Who's got a bottle? Somebody took a cork out of a bottle. Who was it? Say, Will, have you got a bottle?"

"Thought you said that your doctor told you not to drink."

"He did; he said that I had intercostal rheumatism. He examined me carefully, and when I asked him what he thought, he replied, 'Mr. Flummers, you can't afford to drink.'"

"And did you tell him that you could afford it—that it didn't cost you anything?"

"Oh, ho, ho, no! Say, send out and get a bottle. What are you fellows playing there? Ten cents ante, all jack pots? It's a robbers' game."

*   *   *   *   *

In every community a stranger wearing black whiskers was under suspicion. A detective shrewdly suggested that the murderer might have shaved, and he claimed great credit for this timely hint; but no matter, the search for the black-whiskered man was continued. Dave Kittymunks was arrested in all parts of the country, and the head-line writer, whose humor could not long be held in subjection, began to express himself thus: "Dave Kittymunks captured in St. Paul, also seized in New Orleans, and is hotly pursued in the neighborhood of Kansas City."

Witherspoon, sitting by his library fire at night, would say over and over again: "I told him never to keep any money in the house. He was so close, so suspicious; and then to put his money in a safe that a boy might have knocked to pieces!" And it became Mrs. Witherspoon's habit to declare: "I just know that somebody will break into our house next." Then the merchant's impatience would express itself with a grunt. "Oh, it has given you and Ellen a rare chance for speculation. We'd better wall ourselves in a cave and die there waiting for robbers to drill their way in. It does seem to me that they ought to catch that fellow, I told Brooks that he'd better increase the reward to fifty thousand."

Witherspoon and Brooks called at Henry's office. "You may publish the fact that I have offered fifty thousand dollars reward for Kittymunks," said Brooks, speaking to Henry, but looking into the room where Miss Drury was at work.

"That ought to be a great stimulus," Henry replied, "but it doesn't appear to me that there has been any lack of effort."

"No," said Witherspoon; "but the prospect of fifty thousand dollars will make a strong effort stronger."

"By the way," Henry remarked, "this is the first time you have visited me in my work-room."

Witherspoon replied: "Yes, that's so; and it strikes me that you might get more comfortable quarters."

"Comfortable enough for a workshop," Henry rejoined.

"Yes, I presume so. Are you ready, Brooks?"

"Yes, sir."

"We have just come from police headquarters," said Witherspoon, "and thought that we would stop and tell you of the increased reward. You were late at dinner yesterday. Will you be on time this evening?"

"Yes, I think so."

When they were gone, Henry went into Miss Drury's room. "Was that your father?" she asked.

"Yes."

"And he scolded you for being late yesterday. If he had suspected that I was the cause, I suppose he would have come in and stormed at me."

"You were not the cause."

"Yes, you were helping me with my work."

"It was my work, too." He tilted a pile of newspapers off a chair, sat down and said: "I feel at home with you."

"Oh, am I so homely?" she asked, smiling.

"Yes, restoring the word to its best meaning. By the way, you haven't cut off your hair."

"No, I forgot it, but I'm going to."

"My sister Ellen has hair something like yours, but not so heavy and not so bright."

"I should like to see her."

"Because she has hair like yours?"

"What a question! No, because I am acquainted with her brother, of course."

"And when you become acquainted with a man do you want to meet his sister?"

"Oh, you are getting to be a regular tease, Mr. Witherspoon. After awhile I shall be afraid to talk to you."

"I hope the clock will refuse to record that time. You say that you would like to see my sister. You shall see her; you must come home to dinner with me."

She gave him a quick look, a mere glance, the shortest sentence within the range of human expression, but in that short sentence a full book of meaning. One moment she was nothing but a resentment; but when she looked up again the light in her eyes had been softened by that half-sarcastic pity which a well-bred woman feels for the ignorance of man.

"Your sister has not called on me," she said.

He replied: "I beg your pardon for overlooking the ceremonious flirtation which women insist shall be indulged in, for I assure you that their ways are sometimes a mystery to me; but I admit that the commonest sort of sense should have kept me from falling into this error. My sister shall call on you."

"Pardon me, but she must not."

"And may I ask why not?"

"My aunt lives in a flat," she answered.

"Suppose she does? What difference can that make?"

"It makes this difference: Your sister couldn't conceal the air of a patron, and I couldn't hide my resentment; therefore," she added with a smile that brought back all her brightness, "to be friends we must remain strangers."

"But suppose I should call on you; would you regard it as a patronage?"

"No."

"Why not?"

"Because you are a man."

"You women are peculiar creatures."

"An old idea always patly expressed," she replied.

"But isn't it true?"

"It must be, or it wouldn't have lived so long," she answered.

"A pleasing sentiment," he replied, "but old age is not a mark of truth, for nothing is grayer than falsehood."

"But it finally dies, and truth lives on," she rejoined.

"No, it is often buried."

"So is a mummy buried, but it is brought to light again."

"Yes, but it doesn't live; it is simply a mummy."

"Oh, well," she said, "I know that you are wrong, but I won't worry with it."

John Richmond opened the door of Henry's room. "Come in," Henry called, advancing to meet him. "How are you? And now that you are here, make yourself at home."

"All right," Richmond replied, sitting down, reaching out with his foot and drawing a spittoon toward him. "How is everything running?"

"First-rate."

"You are getting out a good paper. I have just heard that the reward for Kittymunks has been increased."

"Yes, it was increased not more than an hour ago."

"Who is to pay it?"

"The State, you know, has offered a small reward; the Colossus Company is to pay twenty thousand dollars, and the remainder will be paid by the Colton estate."

"Who constitutes the Colton estate?"

"Brooks, mainly."

Richmond put his hand to his mouth. "That's what I thought," said he. "Do you know Brooks very well?" he asked after a short silence.

"Not very."

"What do you think of him?"

"I despise him."

"I thought so. As the French say, whom does it benefit?"

They looked at each other, but said nothing. There could be no mistake as to who was benefited. After a time Henry remarked: "I see that Flummers has gone to Omaha to identify a suspect."

"He did go, but I heard some of the boys say that he returned this morning. Is your work all done for to-day?"

"Yes, about all."

"Suppose we go over to the club."

"All right. Wait a moment."

Henry stepped into Miss Drury's room. "You must; forgive me," he said, in a low tone.

"What for?" she asked, in surprise.

"For so rudely inviting you to dinner when my sister had not even called on you."

"Oh, that's nothing," she replied, laughing. "Such mistakes are common enough with men, I should think."

"Not with sensible men. What have you here?"

"Oh, some stupid paragraphs about women."

"They'll keep till to-morrow."

"But Mr. Mitchell said he wanted them to-day."

"Tell him if he calls for them that I want them to-morrow. You'd better go home and rest."

"Rest? Why, I haven't done anything to make me tired."

"Well, you don't know how soon you may be tired, and you'd better take your rest in advance. All right, John," he said in a louder tone, "I'm with you."

When they entered the office of the Press Club, a forensic voice, followed by laughter, bore to them the intelligence that Mr. Flummers was in the front room, declaiming his recent adventures. They found the orator measuredly stepping the short distance between this round table and the post on which was fixed the button of the electric bell. Led by fondness to believe that some one, moved to generosity, might ask him to ring for the drinks, he showed a disposition to loiter whenever he reached the post, and the light of eager expectancy and the shadow of sore disappointment played a trick pantomime on his countenance.

"Oh, ho, ho, here come two of my staff. John, I have been talking for an hour, and the bell is rusting from disuse."

"Why don't you ring it on your own account?"

"Oh, no; you can't expect one man to do everything."

"Go on with your story."

"But is there anything in it?"

"If you mean your story, I don't think there's much in it."

"If you cut it short enough," said Mortimer, "we'll all contribute."

"There spoke a disgruntled Englishman," Flummers exclaimed. "Having no humor himself, he scowls on the— the"—He scalloped the air, but it failed to bring the right word. "Jim, you'd better confine yourself to the writing of encyclopedias and not meddle with the buzz-saw of—of sharp retort."

"He appears to have made it that time," said Whittlesy.

"Now, Whit, it may behoove some men to speak, but it doesn't behoove you. Remember that I hold you in the hollow of my hand."

"Let us have the story," said Henry.

"But is the laborer worthy of his hire—is there anything in it?"

"Yes, ring the bell."

"That's the stuff."

"Flummers," some one remarked, a few moments later, "I don't think that I ever saw you drunk."

Flummers tapped his forehead and replied: "The brain predominates the jag. But I must gather up the flapping ends of my discourse. I will begin again."

"Are you going to repeat that dose of bloody rot?" Mortimer asked.

"Jim, I pity you. I pity any man that can't see a point when it's held under his nose."

"Or smell one when it's held under his eye," someone suggested.

"You fellows are pretty gay," said Flummers. "You must have drawn your princely stipends this week." He hesitated a moment, pressed his hand to his forehead, cut a fish-hook in the air and resumed his recital:

"When I reached Omaha it was snowing. The heavens wore a feathery frown."

"He didn't fill," said Whittlesy.

Flummers condemned him with a look and continued: "The wind whetted itself to keenness on a bleak knob and came down to shave its unhappy customers."

"He made his flush," said Whittlesy.

Flummers did not look at him. "I went immediately to the jail, where one of the rank and file of the Kittymunkses was confined; and say, you ought to have seen the poor, miserable, bug-bitten wretch they stood up in front of me. He wore about a half-pint of dirty whiskers, and in his make-up he reminded me of a scare-crow that brother and I once made to put out on the farm in Wisconsin. I have seen a number of Kittymunkses, but he was the worst. I said, 'Say, why don't you wash yourself?' and the horrible suggestion made him shudder. 'Is this the man?' the sheriff asked. 'Gentlemen,' I replied, disdaining the sheriff, 'on the first train that pulls out I am going back to Chicago; and whenever you catch another baboon that has worn himself threadbare by sitting around your village, telegraph me and I will come and tell you to turn him loose.' 'Then he is not the man?' said the sheriff, giving me a look that told of deep official disappointment. 'Gentlemen,' I replied, still disdaining the sheriff, 'I never saw this poor wretch before. Tra la.' I met one gentleman in the town. I think he belonged to the sporting fraternity. He said, 'Will you have something?' and we went into a place kept by a retired prize-fighter. My friend pointed to a noisy party at the rear end of the room, and said: 'The city authorities.' 'Should they live?' I asked, and my friend said, 'They should not.' And then papa was in town. 'Make me a sufficient inducement,' said I, 'and I will take a position on one of your newspapers and kill them off. One of my specialties is the killing of city authorities. Nature has intended them for my meat. I have killed mayors in nearly every place that is worthy of the name of municipality; and between the ordinary city official and papa,' I added, 'there is about as much affinity as there is between a case of hydrophobia and a limpid trout stream trickling its way through the woods of my native Wisconsin.' Say, do you know what he did? He eyed me suspiciously and edged off toward the door. Oh, it is painful to stand by helplessly and see fate constantly casting my lot among jays."

"Mr. Flummers, do you think that you would recognize Kittymunks if you were to see him?" Henry asked.

"Sure thing. Papa's friends may deceive him, but his eyes, backed by his judgment, never do. Say, I'm getting up a great scheme, and pretty soon I'm going to travel through the country with it. I'm going to organize an investment company for country merchants. I've already got about fifteen thousand dollars' worth of stock ready to issue. Has everybody been to lunch? I have been so busy that I haven't eaten anything since early this morning. Joe, lend me fifty cents."

"And take a mortgage on your investment company?"

"Oh, ho, ho, that's a good thing. The other day one of your so-called literary men said that he would give me two dollars an hour to write for him from dictation. 'Ha, I've struck a soft thing,' thinks I, and I goes to his den with him. Well, when I had worked about half an hour, taking down his guff, he turns to me and says, 'Say, lend me a dollar.' 'I haven't got but forty cents,' I replied. But he didn't weaken. 'Well, let me have that,' says he. 'You've got job and I haven't, you know.' And he robbed me. I've got to go out now and see a business jay from Peoria. With my newspaper work and my side speculations I'm kept pretty busy. Joe, where's that fifty?"

"Gave it to you a moment ago."

"All right. Say, will you fellows be here when I come back?"

"Not if we can get out," Whittlesy replied.

"Oh, you've bobbed up again, have you? But remember that papa holds you in the hollow of his hand."

CHAPTER XX

CRIED A SENSATION

In Chicago was a sheet—it could not be called a newspaper and assuredly was not a publication—that was rarely seen until late at night, and which always appeared to have been smuggled across the border-line of darkness into the light of the street lamps. Ragged boys, carrying this sheet, hung about the theaters and cried a sensation when the play was done. Their aim was to catch strangers, and to turn fiercely upon their importunity was not so effective as simply to say, "I live here."

One night, as Henry and Ellen came out of a theater, they heard these ragged boys shouting the names of Witherspoon and Brooks.

"Gracious," said Ellen, with sudden weight on Henry's arm, "what does that mean?"

"It's nothing but a fake," he answered.

"But get a paper and see; won't you?"

"Yes, as soon as I can."

They were so crowd-pressed that it was some time before they could reach one of the boys; and when they did, Ellen snatched a paper and attempted to read it by the light of the carriage lamp.

"Wait until we get home," he said. "I tell you it amounts to nothing."

"No, we will go to a restaurant," she replied.

The sensation was a half column of frightening head on a few inches of smeared body. It declared that recent developments pointed to the fact that Witherspoon and Brooks knew more concerning the whereabouts of Dave Kittymunks than either of them cared to tell. It was known that old Colton's extreme conservatism had been regarded as an obstruction, and that while they might not actually have figured in the murder, yet they were known to be pleased at the result, that the large reward was all a "bluff," and that it was to their interest to aid the escape of Kittymunks.

Before breakfast the next morning Brooks was at Witherspoon's house. A "friend" had called his attention to the article. Had it appeared in one of the reputable journals instead of in this fly-by-night smircher of the characters of men, a suit for criminal libel would have been brought, but to give countenance to this slander was to circulate it; and therefore the two men were resolved not to permit the infamy to place them under the contribution of a moment's worry.

"The character of a successful man is a target to be shot at by the envious," said Witherspoon. He was pacing the room, and anger had hardened his step. "A target to be shot at," he repeated, "and the shots are free."

"I didn't know what to do," Brooks replied. He stood on the hearth-rug with his hands behind him. "I was so worried that I couldn't sleep after I saw the thing late last night; and my wife was crying when I left home."

"Infamous scoundrels!" Witherspoon muttered.

"I didn't think anything could be done," Brooke continued, "but I thought it best to see you at once."

"Of course," said Witherspoon.

"But, after all, don't you think we ought to have those wretches locked up?" Brooke asked.

"Yes," Witherspoon answered, "and we ought to have them hanged, but we might as well set out to look for Kittymunks. Ten chances to one they are not here at all; the thing might have been printed in a town three hundred miles from here."

"Yes, that's so," Brooks admitted; and addressing Henry, who stood at a window, gazing out, he added: "What do you think about it?"

Henry did not heed the question, so forgetfully was he gazing, and Brooks repeated it.

"If you have decided not to worry," Henry answered, "it is better not to trouble yourselves at all. I doubt whether you could ever find the publishers of the paper."

"You are right," Brooks agreed.

"Character used to be regarded as something at least half way sacred," said Witherspoon, "but now, like an old plug hat, it is kicked about the streets. And yet we boast of our freedom. Freedom, indeed! So would it be freedom to sit at a window and shoot men as they pass. I swear to God that I never had as much trouble and worry as I've had lately. *Everything* goes wrong. What about Jordway & Co., of Aurora?"

"Oh, I forgot to tell you," Brooks answered. "Jordway has killed himself, and the affairs of the firm are in a hopeless tangle."

"Of coarse," Witherspoon replied, "and we'll never get a cent."

"I'm afraid not, sir. I cautioned you against them, you remember."

"Never saw anything like it," Witherspoon declared, not recalling the caution that Brooks had advised, or not caring to acknowledge it.

"Oh, everything may come out all right. Pardon me, Mr. Witherspoon, but I think you need rest"

"There is no rest," Witherspoon replied.

"And yet," said Henry, turning from the window, "you took me to task for saying that I sometimes felt there was nothing in the entire scheme of life."

"For saying it at your age, yes. You have but just begun to try life and have no right to condemn it."

"I didn't condemn it without a hearing. Isn't there something wrong when the poor are wretched and the rich are miserable?"

"Nonsense," said Witherspoon.

"Oh, but that's no argument."

"Isn't it? Well, then there shall be none."

"I must be getting back," said Brooks.

"Won't you stay to breakfast?" Witherspoon asked. "It will be ready in a few minutes. Hum"—looking at his watch—"ought to have been ready long ago. Everything goes wrong. Can't even get anything to eat. I'll swear I never saw the like."

"I'm much obliged, but I can't stay," Brooks answered.

"Well, I suppose I shall be down to the store some time to-day. If anybody calls to see me, just say that I am at home, standing round begging for something to eat. Good morning."

Henry laughed, and the merchant gave him a strained look. For a moment the millionaire bore a striking likeness to old Andrew, at the time when he declared that the devil had gone wrong. The young man sought to soothe him when Brooks was gone; he apologized for laughing; he said that he keenly felt that there was cause for worry, but that the picture of a Chicago merchant standing about at home begging for his breakfast, while important business awaited him at the store, was enough to crack the thickest crust of solemnity. The merchant's dignity was soon brought back; never was it far beyond his reach. At breakfast he was severe with silence.

Over and over again during the day Henry repeated Richmond's words, "Whom does it benefit" and these words went to bed with him, and as though restless, they turned and tossed themselves upon his mind throughout the night, and like children, they clamored to be taken up at early morning, to be dressed in the many colors of supposition.

CHAPTER XXI

A HELPLESS OLD WOMAN

In Kansas City was arrested a suspicious-looking man, who, upon being taken to jail, confessed that his name was Dare Kittymunks and owned that he had killed old man Colton. Thus was ended the search for the murderer, the newspapers said, and the vigilance of the Kansas City police was praised. But it soon transpired that the prisoner had been a street preacher in Topeka at the time when the murder was committed, that he had on that day created a sensation by announcing himself John the Baptist and swearing that all other Johns the Baptist were base impostors. The fellow was taken to an asylum for the insane, and the search for Dave Kittymunks was resumed.

Old Mrs. Colton had not moved a muscle since the night of the murder. She lay looking straight at the ceiling, and in her eyes was an expression that seemed constantly to repeat, "My body is dead, but my mind is alive." Once every week the pastor of her church came to see her. He was an old man, threatened with palsy, and had long ago ceased to find pleasure in the appetites and vanities of this life. He came on Sunday, just before the time for evening services in the church, and kneeling at the old woman's chair, which he placed near her bedside, lifted his shaking voice in prayer. It was a touching sight, one infirmity pleading for another, palsy praying for paralysis; but upon these devotions Brooks began to look with a frown.

"What is the use of it?" he asked, speaking to his wife. "If a celebrated specialist can't do her any good, I know that an old man's prayer can't."

"We ought not to deny her anything," the wife answered.

"And we ought not to inflict her with anything," the husband replied.

"Prayer was never an infliction to her."

"But this old man's praying is an infliction to the rest of us."

"Not to me; and you needn't hear him."

"I can't help it if I'm at home."

"But you needn't be at home when he comes."

"Oh, I suppose I could go over and stand on the lake shore, but it would be rather unpleasant this time of year."

"There are other places you can go."

"Oh, I suppose so. Doesn't make any difference to you, of course, where I go."

"Not much," she answered.

The Witherspoon family was gathered one evening in the mother's room. It was Mrs. Witherspoon's birthday, and it was a home-like picture, this family group, with the mother sitting in a rocking-chair, fondly looking about and giving the placid heed of love to Henry whenever he spoke. On the walls were hung the portraits of early Puritans, the brave and rugged ancestors of Uncle Louis and Uncle Harvey, and all her mother's people, who were dark.

Ellen had been imitating a Miss Miller, who, it was said, was making a determined set at Henry, and Witherspoon was laughing at the aptness of his daughter's mimicry.

"I must confess," said Mrs. Witherspoon, slowly rocking herself, "that I don't see anything to laugh at. Miss Miller is an exceedingly nice girl, I'm sure, but I don't think she is at all suited to my son. She giggles at everything, and Henry is too sober-minded for that sort of a wife."

"But marriage would probably cure her giggling," Witherspoon replied, slyly winking at Henry. "To a certain kind of a girl there is nothing that so inspires a giggle as the prospect of marriage, but marriage itself is the greatest of all soberers—it sometimes removes all traces of the previous intoxication."

"Now, George, what is the use of talking that way?" She rarely called him George. "You know as well as you know anything that I didn't giggle. Of course I was lively enough, but I didn't go about giggling as Miss Miller does."

"Oh, perhaps not exactly as Miss Miller does, but"—

"George!"

"I say you didn't. But anybody can see that Ellen is a sensible girl, and yet she giggles."

"Not at the prospect of marriage, papa," the girl replied. "To look at Mr. Brooks and his wife is quite enough to make me serious."

"Brooks and his wife? What do you mean?"

"Perhaps I oughtn't to have said anything, but they appear to make each other miserable. There, now, I wish I *hadn't* said anything. I might have known that it would make you look glum."

"How do you know that they make each other miserable?"

"I know this, that when they should be on their good behavior they can't keep from snapping at each other. I was over there this afternoon, and when Mr. Brooks came home he began to growl about the preacher's coming once a week to pray for Mrs. Colton. He ought to be ashamed of himself. The poor old creature lies there so helpless; and he wants to deny her even the consolation of hearing her pastor's voice. And he knows that she was so devoted to the church."

"My daughter," Witherspoon gravely said, "there must be some mistake about this."

"But I know that there isn't any mistake about it. I was there, I tell you."

"And still there may be some mistake," Witherspoon insisted.

"What doctor's treating the old lady?" Henry asked.

"A celebrated specialist, Brooks tells me," Witherspoon answered.

"What's his name?"

Opie Read

"I don't remember," said Witherspoon. "Do you know, Ellen?"

"Doctor Linmarck," Ellen answered.

"Let us not think of anything so very unpleasant," said Mrs. Witherspoon.

But the spirit of pleasantry was flown. With another imitation of Miss Miller, Ellen strove to call it back, but failed, for Witherspoon paid no attention to her. He sat brooding, with a countenance as fixed as the expression of a mask, and in his gaze, bent on that nothing through which nothing can be seen, there was no light.

"Father, do your new slippers fit?" Mrs. Witherspoon asked. He was not George now.

"Very nicely," he answered, with a warning absentmindedness. Presently he went to the library, and shutting out the amenities of that cheerful evening, shut in his own somber brooding.

"I don't see why he should let that worry him so," said Mrs. Witherspoon. "He's getting to be so sensitive over Brooks."

"I don't think it's his sensitiveness over Brooks, mother," Ellen replied, "but the fact that he is gradually finding out that Brooks is not so perfect as he pretends to be."

"I don't know," the mother rejoined, "but I think he has just as much confidence in Brooks as he ever had. I know he said last night that the Colossus couldn't get along without him."

"Ellen," said Henry, "what is the name of that doctor?"

"Linmarck. It isn't so hard to remember, is it?"

"No, but I forgot it."

Immediately after reaching the office the next day, Henry sent for a reporter who had lived so long in Chicago that he was supposed thoroughly to know the city.

"Are you acquainted with Doctor Linmarck?" Henry asked when the reporter entered the room.

"Linmarck? Let me see. No, don't think I am."

"Did you ever hear of him?"

"What's his particular line?"

"Paralysis, I think."

"No, I've never heard of him."

"Well, find out all you can about him and let me know as soon as possible. And say," he added as the reporter turned to go, "don't say a word about it."

"All right."

Several hours later the reporter returned. "Did you learn anything?" Henry asked.

"Yes, about all there is to learn, I suppose. He has an office on Wabash Avenue, near Twelfth Street. I called on him."

"Does he look like a great specialist?"

"Well, his beard is hardly long enough for a great specialist."

"But does he appear to be prosperous?"

"His location stands against that supposition."

"But does he strike you as being an impostor?"

"Well, not exactly that; but I shouldn't like to be paralyzed merely to give him a chance to try his hand on me. I told him that I had considerable trouble with my left arm, and he asked if I had ever been afflicted with rheumatism, or if I had ever been stricken with typhoid fever, or—I don't remember how many diseases he tried on suspicion. I told him that so far as I knew I had been in excellent health, and then he began to ask me about my parents. I told him that they were dead and that I didn't care to be treated for any disease that they might have had. I asked him where he was from, and he said Philadelphia. He hasn't been here long, but is treating some very prominent people, he says. There may be a reason why he should be employed, but I failed to find it."

CHAPTER XXII

TO GO ON A VISIT

A month must have passed since Henry had sought to investigate the standing of Dr. Linmarck, when, one evening, Ellen astonished her father with the news that old Mrs. Colton was to be taken on a visit to her sister, who lived in New Jersey. The sister had written an urgent letter to Mrs. Brooks, begging that the old lady might straightway be sent to her, and offering to relieve Mr. Brooks of all the trouble and responsibility that might be incurred by the journey. She would send her son and her family physician. Witherspoon grunted at so absurd a request and was surprised that Brooks should grant it. The old woman might die on the train, and besides, what possible pleasure could she extract from such a visit? It was nonsense.

"But suppose the poor old creature wants to go?" said Mrs. Witherspoon.

"Ah, but how is any one to know whether she does or not?"

"Of course no one can tell what she thinks, but it is reasonable to suppose that she would like to see her sister."

"Oh, yes, it is reasonable to suppose almost anything when

you start out on that line; but it's not common sense to act upon almost any supposition. Of course, the old lady can live but a short time, and I think that if she were given her own choice she would prefer to die in her own bed. I shall advise Brooks not to let her go."

"I hope you'll not do that," said Henry, and he spoke with an eagerness that caused the merchant to give him a look of sharp inquiry. "I hope that you'll not seek to deprive the sister, who I presume is a very old woman, of the pleasure of sheltering one so closely related to her. The trip may be fatal, and yet it might be a benefit. At any rate don't advise Brooks not to let her go."

"Oh, it's nothing to me," Witherspoon replied, "and I didn't suppose that it was so much to the rest of you. How I do miss that old man!" he added after musing for a few moments. "The peculiar laugh he had when pleased became a very distressing cough whenever he fancied that his expenses were running too high, and every day I am startled by some noise that sounds like his hack, hack! And just as frequently I hear his good-humored ha, ha! He had never gone away during the summer, but he told me that this summer he was going to a watering-place and enjoy himself. 'And, Witherspoon,' he said, 'I'm going to spend money right and left.' Picture that old man spending money either right or left. He would have backed out when the time came. Some demand would have kept him at home."

"His will leaves everything to his wife, I believe," Henry remarked.

"Yes, with the proviso that at her death it is to go to Mrs. Brooks. Brooks has already taken Colton's place in the store, and now the question is, Who can fill Brooks' place?"

"I don't think you will have any trouble in filling it," Henry replied. "No matter who drops out, the affairs of this life go on just the same. A man becomes so identified with a business that people think it couldn't be run without him. He dies, and the business—improves."

"Yes, it appears so," Witherspoon admitted; "but what I wanted to get at, coming straight to the point, is this: I need you now more than ever before. One of the penalties of wealth is that a rich man is forced constantly to fumble about in the dark, feeling for some one whose touch may inspire confidence. That's the position I'm in."

"You make a strong appeal," said Henry, "far stronger than any personal advantages you could point out to me."

"But is it strong enough to move you?"

"It might be strong enough to move me to a sacrifice of myself, and still fail to draw me into a willingness to risk the opinion you have expressed of what you term my manliness. As a business man I know that I should be a failure, and then I'd have your pity instead of your good opinion. Let me tell you that I am a very ordinary man. I haven't the quickness which is a business man's enterprise, nor that judgment which is his safeguard. My newspaper is a success, but it is mainly because I have a capable man in the business office. It grieves me to disappoint you, and I will take an oath that if I felt myself capable I'd cheerfully give up journalism and place myself at your service."

"Father," said Mrs. Witherspoon—and anxiously she had been watching her husband—"I don't see what more he could say."

"He has said quite enough," Witherspoon replied.

"But you are not angry, are you, papa?" Ellen asked.

"No, I'm hurt."

"I'm very sorry," said Henry, "but permit me to say that a man of your strength of mind shouldn't be hurt by a present disappointment that may serve to prevent a possible calamity in the future."

"High-sounding nonsense. I could pick up almost any bootblack and make a good business man of him."

"But you can't pick up almost any boy and make a good bootblack of him. The bootblack is already a business man in embryo."

Witherspoon did not reply to this statement. He mused for a few moments and then remarked: "If it weren't too late we might make a preacher of you."

Mrs. Witherspoon's countenance brightened. "I am sure he would make a good one," she said. "My grandfather was a minister, and we have a book of his sermons now, some-where. If you want it, my son, I will get it for you."

"Not to-night, mother."

"I didn't mean to-night. Ellen, what *are* you giggling at?"

"Why, mother, he would rather smoke that old black pipe than to read any book that was ever printed."

"When I saw the pipe that had robbed Kittymunks of his coat," said Henry, "I thought of my pipe tied with a ribbon."

During the remainder of the evening Witherspoon joined not

in the conversation, he sat brooding, and when bed-time came, he stood in his accustomed place on the hearth-rug and wound his watch, still appearing to gaze at something far away.

Opie Read

CHAPTER XXIII

HENRY'S INCONSISTENCY

Snorting March came as if blown in off the icy lake, and oozy April fell from the clouds. How weary we grow of winter in a cold land, and how loath is winter to permit the coming of spring! May stole in from the south. There came a warm rain, and the next morning strips of green were stretched along the boulevards.

Nature had unrolled double widths of carpet during the night, and at sunset a yellow button lay where the ground had been harsh so long—a dandelion. An old man, in whom this blithe air stirred a recollection of an amative past, sat on a bench in the park, watching the flirtations of thrill-blooded youth, and pale mothers, housed so long with fretful children, turned loose their cares upon the grass. It was a lolling-time, a time to lose one's self in the blue above, or sweetly muse over the green below.

One night a hot wind came, and the nest morning was summer. The horse that had drawn coal during the winter, now hitched to an ice wagon, died in the street. The pavements throbbed, the basement restaurants exhaled a sickening air, and through the grating was blown the cellar's cool and mouldy breath; and the sanitary writer on the editorial page cried out: "Boil your drinking-water!"

It was Witherspoon's custom, during the heated term, to take his wife and his daughter to the seaside, and to return when the weather there became insufferably hot. It was supposed that Henry would go, but when the time came he declared that he had in view a piece of work that most not be neglected. Witherspoon recognized the urgency of no work except his own. "What, you can't go!" he exclaimed. "What do you mean by 'can't go'?"

"I mean simply that it is not convenient for me to get away at this time."

"And is it your scheme now to act entirely upon your own convenience? Can't you sometimes pull far enough away from yourself to forget your own convenience?"

"Oh, yes, but I can't very well forget that on this occasion it is almost impossible for me to get away. Of course you don't understand this, and I am afraid that if I should try I couldn't make it very clear to you."

"Oh, you needn't make any explanation to me, I assure you. I had planned an enjoyment for your mother and sister, and if you desire to interfere with it, I have nothing more to say."

"I have no business that shall interfere with their enjoyment," Henry replied. "I'm ready to go at any time."

The next day Witherspoon said: "Henry, if you have decided to go, there is no use of my leaving home."

"Now there's no need of all this sacrifice," Mrs. Witherspoon protested, "for the truth is I don't want to go anyway. During the hot weather I am never so comfortable anywhere as I am at home. My son, you shall not go on my account; and as for Ellen, she can go with some of our friends. But, father, I do think that you need rest."

"Very true," he admitted, "but unfortunately we can't drop a worry and run away from it."

"But what is worrying you now?"

"*Everything*. Nothing goes on as it should, and every day it seems that a new annoyance takes hold of me."

"In your time you have advised many a man to be sensible," said Henry, "and now if you please, permit a man who has never been very sensible to advise you." Witherspoon looked at him. "My advice is, be sensible."

In a fretful resentment Witherspoon jerked his shoulder as if with muscular force he sought a befitting reply, but he said nothing and Henry continued: "This may be impudence on my part, but in impudence there may lie a good intention and a piece of advice that may not be bad. The worry of a strong man is a sign of danger. The truth is that if you keep on this way you'll break down."

"None of you know what you are talking about," Witherspoon declared. "I'm as strong as I ever was. I'm simply annoyed, that's all."

"Why don't you see the doctor?" his wife asked.

"What do I want to see him for? What does he know about it? Don't you worry. I'm all right."

His fretfulness was not continuous. Sometimes his spirits rose to exceeding liveliness, and then he laughed at the young man and joked him about Miss Miller. But a single word, however lightly spoken, served to turn him back to peevishness. One evening Henry remarked that he was compelled to leave town on the day following and that he might be absent nearly a week.

"Why, how is this?" Witherspoon asked, with a sudden change of manner. "The other day you almost swore that it was impossible for you to leave home, and now you are compelled to go. What do you mean?"

"I have business out of town, and it demands my attention."

"*Business* out of town. The other day you despised business; now you've got business out of town. I'll take an oath right now that you are the strangest mortal I ever struck."

"I admit the appearance of inconsistency," Henry replied.

"And I *know* the existence of it," Witherspoon rejoined.

"You think so. The truth is that the affair I now have on hand had something to do with my objecting to leave town last week."

"Why don't you tell me what it is?"

"I will when the time is ripe."

The merchant grunted. "Is it a love affair?"

Mrs. Witherspoon became newly concerned. "In one sense, yes," Henry answered. "It is the love of justice."

Witherspoon called his wife's attention by clearing his throat.

"Madam, I may be wrong, but it strikes me that your son is crazy. Good night."

Henry left town the next morning. He went to New Jersey.

CHAPTER XXIV

WORE A ROSE ON HIS COAT

Henry was absent nearly a week, and upon returning he did not refer to the business that had so peremptorily called him away. Mrs. Witherspoon still had a fear that it might be a love affair, and Ellen had a fear that it might not be. To keep the young woman's interest alive a mystery was necessary, and to free the mother's love from anxiety unrestrained frankness was essential. And so there was not enough of mystery to thrill the girl nor enough of frankness to satisfy the mother. In this way a week was passed.

"I don't see why you make so much of it," Witherspoon said to his wife. "Is there anything so strange in a young man's leaving town? Do you expect him to remain forever within calling distance? He told you that you should know in due time. What more can you ask? You are foolishly worried over him, and what is there to worry about?"

"I suppose I am," she answered, "but I'm so much afraid that he'll marry some girl that I shall not like."

"It's not only that, Caroline. You are simply afraid that he will marry some girl. The fear of not liking her is a secondary anxiety."

"But, father, you know"—

"Oh, yes, I know. But he is a man—presumably," he added to himself—"and your love cannot make him a child. It is true that we were robbed of the pleasure his infancy would have afforded us, but it's not true that there now exists any way by which that lost pleasure can be supplied. As for myself, I regret the necessity that compels me to say that he is far from being a comfort to me. What has he brought me? Nothing but an additional cause for worry."

"Father, don't say that!"

"But I am compelled to say it. I have pointed out a career to him and he simply bats his eyes at it. He is the most peculiar creature I ever saw. Oh, I know he has gone through enough to make him peculiar; I know all about that, but I don't see the sense of keeping up that peculiarity. He is aimless, and he doesn't want an aim urged upon him."

"But, father, he has made his newspaper a success."

"Ah, but what does it amount to? Within ten years he might make a hundred thousand dollars out of it, but"—

"Oh, surely more than that," she insisted.

"Well, suppose he does make more than that; say that he may make two hundred thousand. And even then what does it amount to in comparison with what I offer?"

"But you know he wants to be independent."

"Independent!" he repeated. "I'll swear I don't understand that sort of independence."

"Well," she said, with a consoling sigh, "it will come out all right after a while."

They were sitting in Mrs. Witherspoon's room. The footman announced that Mr. Brooks was waiting in the library. Witherspoon frowned.

"You needn't see him, dear," said his wife.

"Yes, I will. But I am tired and don't care to discuss business affairs. Of late he brings nothing but bad news."

The manager was exquisitely dressed and wore a rose on the lapel of his coat. "I am on my way to an entertainment at the Yacht Club," said he, when the merchant entered the library, "and I thought I'd drop in for a few moments."

"I'm glad you did," Witherspoon replied. "Sit down."

"I haven't long to stay," said Brooks, seating himself. "I am on one of the committees and must be getting over. Is your son going?"

"I don't know. He hasn't come home yet."

"He was invited," said Brooks.

"That doesn't make any difference," Witherspoon replied. "He appears to pay but little attention to invitations, or to anything else, for that matter. Spends the moat of his time at the Press Club, I think."

"That's singular."

"Very," said Witherspoon.

Opie Read

"I was there the evening they gave a reception to Patti, some time ago," Brooke remarked, "but I didn't see anything so very attractive about the place."

"I suppose not," Witherspoon replied, and then he added: "That's Henry now, I think."

Henry came in and was apparently surprised to see Brooks. "I have been detained on account of business," he remarked as he sat down. Brooks smiled. Evidently he knew what was passing in Witherspoon's mind.

"My affairs may be light to some people," Henry said, "but they are heavy enough to me."

By looking serious Brooks sought to mollify the effect of his smile. He had not taken the time to think that in his sly currying of Witherspoon's favor he might be discovered, but now that he was caught he fell back upon the recourse of a bungling compliment. "Oh, I'm sure," said he, "that your business is most important. Your paper shows the care and ability with which you preside over it. I think it's the best paper in town, and advertisers tell me that they get excellent returns from it." Here he caught Witherspoon's eye and hastened to add: "Still, I believe that your place is with us in the store. You could soon make yourself master of every detail."

"But we will not talk about that now," Witherspoon spoke up.

"Of course not; but I merely mentioned it to show my belief in your son's abilities."

The footman appeared at the door. "Two gentlemen wish to see Mr. Brooks."

"Who are they?" Witherspoon asked.

"Wouldn't give me their names, sir."

"Some of the boys from the club," said Brooks. "Well, I must bid you good evening."

"There was something I wanted to say to you," the merchant remarked, walking down the hall with him.

Henry did not get up, but he listened eagerly. Presently he heard Witherspoon exclaim: "Great God!" And a moment later the merchant came rushing back.

"Where is my hat?" he cried. "Henry, Brooks is arrested on a charge of murdering Colton! Where is my hat?"

Henry got up, placed his hand on Witherspoon's shoulder, and said: "Sit down here, father."

"Sit down the devil!" he raved. "I tell you that Brooks has been arrested. I am going down-town."

"Not to-night. Sit down here."

"What do you mean, sir!"

"I mean that you must not go down-town. You can do no good by going, Brooks is guilty. There is no doubt about it."

The old man dropped in his chair. Mrs. Witherspoon came running into the room. "What on earth is the matter?" she cried. Witherspoon struggled to his feet. Henry caught him by the arm. "Mother, don't be alarmed. Brooks has simply been arrested."

"For the murder of Colton!" Witherspoon hoarsely whispered. His voice had failed him.

"Sit down, mother, and we will talk quietly about it. There is no cause for excitement when you make up your minds that the fellow is guilty, which you must do, for Mrs. Colton has made a statement—she saw Brooks kill the old man."

Witherspoon dropped in his chair. His hands hung listlessly beside him. Mrs. Witherspoon ran to him.

"Father!"

He lifted his hand, a heavy weight it seemed, and motioned her away. "The Colossus is ruined!" he hoarsely whispered. "Ruined. They'll try to mix me up in it. Ruined!"

"You can't be mixed up in it, and the Colossus will not be ruined," Henry replied.

"Yes, ruined. You haven't brought me anything but bad luck."

"I have brought you the best luck of your life. I have helped you to get rid of a vampire."

"You have?" He turned his lusterless eyes upon Henry.

"Yes, I have, and if you will be patient for a few moments I will make it plain to you. But wait, you must not think of going down-town to-night. Will you listen to me?"

"Yes."

"I was not the only one who suspected that Brooks had something to do with the murder. Many people, in fact—it seemed that almost everybody placed him under suspicion. But there was no evidence against him; there was nothing but a strong supposition. You remember one evening not long ago when Ellen said that he objected to the preacher's coming to pray for Mrs. Colton. This was enough to stamp him a brute. Give that sort of a man the nerve and he won't stop short of any cruelty or any crime."

"Are you going to tell me something or do you simply intend to preach?" Witherspoon asked. His voice had returned.

"Father, he's telling you as fast as he can."

"And I must tell it my own way," Henry said. "That same evening I learned the name of the doctor—the great specialist employed by Brooks to treat the old lady. But I inquired about him and found that he was simply a cheap quack. This was additional cause for suspicion. I called on a detective and told him that I suspected Brooks. At this he smiled. Then I said that if he would agree to give half the reward to any charity that I might name, in the event of success, I would submit my plan, and then he became serious. I convinced him that I had not only a plausible but a direct clue, and he agreed to my proposal. I then told him about the doctor; I expressed my belief that the old woman must know something and urged that this might be brought out if we could get her away and place her under the proper treatment. Well, we learned that she had a sister living in New Jersey. The detective went to see her, and you know the result—the old lady's removal. Recently we received word that she was so much improved that she could mumble in a way to be understood, and last week the detective and I went to see her. This was my apparently inconsistent business out of town."

"But tell us what she said," Witherspoon demanded.

"Her deposition is in the hands of the law." He said this with a sly pleasure—Witherspoon had so often spoken of the law as if it were his agent. "I can simply tell you," Henry continued, "that she saw Brooks when he shot the old man."

"But how can that be? Brooks and his wife ran into the room at the same time. They were together."

"Yes, they ran into the room together, and Brooks had presumably just jumped out of bed. But be that as it may, Mrs. Colton saw him when he shot the old man. And if he is guilty, why should you defend him?"

Witherspoon got up. "You are not going down-town, father," his wife pleaded. "George, you must not go!"

"I'm not going, Caroline." He began to walk up and down the room, but not with his wonted firmness of step. They said nothing to him; they let him walk in his troubled silence. Turning suddenly he would sometimes confront Henry and seem about to denounce him; and then he was strong. But the next moment, and as if weakened by an instantaneous failure of vital forces, he would helplessly turn to his wife as though she could give him strength.

"Don't let it worry you so, father," she begged of him; "don't let it worry you so. It will come out all right. Nobody can fasten any blame on you."

"Yes, they will—yes, they will, the wretches. They hate me; they bleed me every chance they get, and now they want to humble me—ruin me. Nobody can ever know what I have gone through. Defend him!" he exclaimed. "I hope they will hang him. I suspected him, and yet I was afraid to, for in some way it seemed to involve me—I don't know how. But I knew that the wretches would fix it up and ruin the Colossus. For weeks and weeks it has been gnawing me like a rat. But what could I do? I was afraid to discharge him. He's got a running tongue. But what have I done?" he violently asked himself. "He took Colton's place—held Colton's interest. I could do nothing. Sometimes I felt that he was surely innocent. But I fancied that I could hear mutterings whenever I passed people in the street, and the rat would begin its gnawing again. He will drag us all down." His voice failed him, and he sank in his chair. "Ruined! The Colossus is ruined!" he hoarsely whispered.

"If you would stop to think," said Henry, "you would know that your trouble is mostly physical. Your nerves are unstrung. The public is not so willing to believe any story that Brooks may tell. The Colossus will not be injured. But I know that you place very little faith in what I say." The merchant looked at him. "But mark my words: Your standing will not be lowered—the Colossus will not show any ill effect. It is too big a concern to be thus ruined. People trade there for bargains, and not out of sentiment. In a short time Brooks will be forgotten. It is perfectly clear to me."

"Is it?" he asked, with eagerness. "Is it clear to you?"

"Yes, perfectly."

"Then make it clear to me. You can't do it, don't you see? You can't do it."

"Yes, he can, father; yes, he can," Mrs. Witherspoon pleaded. "It is perfectly clear to me. You will look at it differently to-morrow. Come, now, and lie down. Sleep will make it clear. Come on, now."

She took hold of his arm. With a helpless trust he looked up at her. "Come on, now." He lifted his heavy hands, got up with difficulty and suffered her to lead him away.

CHAPTER XXV

IMPATIENTLY WAITING

While it was yet dark, and long before the dimply lake had caught a glint from the coming sun, Witherspoon asked for the morning papers. At brief periods of troubled sleep during the night he had fancied that he was reading of the wreck of the Colossus and of his own disgrace: and when he was told that the papers had not come, that it was too early for them, he said: "Don't try to keep them back. I am prepared." He wanted to get up and put on his clothes, but his wife begged him to remain in bed.

"Was the doctor here?" he asked.

"Yes, don't you remember telling him that Brooks had been arrested?"

"No, I don't remember anything but a bad taste in my mouth. I know him; he leaves a bad taste as his visiting-card. What did he say? Wasn't he delighted to have a chance at me?"

"He said that if you keep quiet you will be all right in a day or two."

"Did anybody else come?"

"Yes, I think so."

"Reporters?" he asked.

"Yes, I think so; but Henry saw them."

"Hum! I suppose he will be known now as Witherspoon the detective."

"No; the part he took will be kept a profound secret."

"I hope so; but don't you think he would rather be known as some sort of freak?"

"No, dear. You do him an injustice."

"But does he do me a *justice*? He's got to pay back every cent I advanced on that newspaper deal."

"We will attend to that, father."

"*We* will. You are to have nothing to do with it."

"I mean that he will."

"That's different. I'll take the thing away from him the first thing he knows. I'm tired of his browbeating. Isn't it time for those papers?"

"Not quite."

"Have they stopped printing them? Are they holding back just to worry me now that they've got me down? Where's Henry?"

"He has just gone out to wait for the carrier-boy. He's

coming now, I think."

Henry came in with the morning papers. "What do they say?" Witherspoon eagerly asked. He flounced up, and drawing the covers about him, sat on the edge of the bed.

"I'll see," Henry answered.

"But be quick about it. Great goodness, I can't wait all day."

"There's so much that I can't tell it in a breath."

"But can't you give me the gist of it? Call yourself a news-paper man and can't get at the gist of a thing."

"Be patient a moment and I will read to you."

During more than an hour Witherspoon sat, listening; and when the last paper had been disposed of, he said: "Why, that isn't so bad. They don't mix me up in it after all. What was that? Brooks seems to he wavering and may make a confession? But what will he say? That's the question. What will he say?"

"How can he say anything to hurt you?" Mrs. Wither spoon asked.

"He can't if he sticks to the truth. But will he? He may want to ruin the Colossus. I will not go near him. They may hang him and let him rot. I will not go near him. The truth is, I have been afraid of him. The best of us have cause to fear the man we have placed too much confidence in. Caroline, I'll get up."

"Not now, father. The doctor said you must not get up to-day."

"But does he suppose I'm going to lie here and let the Colossus run wild? Got nobody to help me; nobody."

"I will go down this morning and see that everything starts off all right," said Henry.

"You will? What do you know about it? You could have known all about it, but what do you know now?"

"I should think that the heads of the departments understand their business; and I hope that I can at least represent you for a short time."

"For a short time? Oh, yes, a short time suits you exactly. Ellen could do that, and I'd send her if she were at home." The girl was at Lake Geneva. "Think you can go down and say, 'Wish you would open this door if you please'? Think you can do that?"

The mother put up her hands as though she would protect her son against the merchant's feelingless reproach. For a time Henry sat looking hard in Witherspoon's blood-shot eyes; and a thought, hot and anger-edged, strove for utterance, but an appealing gesture, a look from that gentle woman, turned his resentment into these consoling words, "Don't worry. I think I know my duty when it's put before me. The Colossus shall not suffer."

How tenderly she looked at him. She made a magnanimity of the cooling of his resentment and she gave him that sacred reward—a mother's gratefulness.

"All right," said the merchant, "Do the best you can."

His quick discernment had caught the play between Henry and Mrs. Witherspoon. "Of course I don't expect you to take my place. I want you merely to show that the Witherspoon family hasn't run away."

The doctor called and found his patient much improved. "A little rest is all you need to bring you about again," the physician said. "Your unsettled nerves have made you morbid. Don't worry. Everything will be all right."

The newspaper reports of the arrest of Brooks, although they proceeded to arraign and condemn him, had on Witherspoon's nervous system more of a retoning effect than could have been brought about by a doctor's skill. That Brooks might be guilty, had not been the merchant's fear; but that he himself might in some way be implicated, had been his morbid dread. Now he could begin to recognize the truth that with a black beast of his own creation he had frightened himself; and he laughed with a nervous shudder. But when the doctor was gone he again became anxious.

"Caroline, didn't he ask if there had ever been any insanity in my family?"

"Why, no; he didn't hint at such a thing."

"I must have dreamed it, then. But what makes me dream such strange things? I thought you told him that my father had been a little off at times. Didn't you?"

"Why, of course not. You never told me that there was ever anything wrong with your father, and even if there was how should I know it?"

"But there wasn't anything wrong with him, Caroline, and why should you say 'if there was.'"

"Now, father, I never thought of such a thing as suspecting

that there was, and please don't let that worry you."

"I won't, but didn't Henry bring a paper and keep it hidden until after I went to sleep?"

"No, he read them all to you."

"I thought he brought in a weekly paper and read something about a widow from Washington."

"No, he didn't."

After a time he dozed and then he began to mutter: "It is easier to pay than to explain."

"What is it, dear?" she asked, not noticing that he dozed.

"Did you speak to me?" he inquired, rousing himself.

"You said something about it's being easier to pay than to explain," she answered.

"Did I? Must have been dreaming. Has Ellen come home?"

"Not yet, but I'm looking for her. Of course she started for home as soon as she could after hearing the news."

"What time is it?"

"Twenty minutes of four," she answered, glancing at the clock.

"I wonder why Henry doesn't come."

"He'll be here soon."

"Has any one heard from Mrs. Brooks?"

"No. I would have gone over there, but I couldn't leave you."

"You are a noble woman, Caroline." She was arranging his pillow and he was looking up at her. "You are too good for me."

"Please don't say that," she pleaded.

"I might as well say it as to feel it. Isn't it time for Henry to come?"

"Yes, I think so. He'll be here soon, I'm sure."

"I hope I shan't have to lie here to-morrow. I can't, and that's all there is about it."

He lay listening with the nervous ear of eagerness until so wearied by disappointing noises that he sank into another doze.

CHAPTER XXVI

TOLD IT ALL

Witherspoon started. "Ah, it's you. Did you bring the evening papers?"

"Yes, here they are," Henry answered.

"What do they say? Can't you tell me? Got the papers and can't tell me what they say?"

"They say a great deal," Henry replied. "Brooks has made a confession."

In an instant Witherspoon sat on the edge of the bed, with the covers jerked about him. He opened his mouth, but no word came forth.

"When he was told that Mrs. Colton had made a statement he gave up," said Henry. "The confession is not a written one, but is doubtless much fuller than if it were. I will take the *Star's* report. They are all practically the same, but this one has a few pertinent questions. I will skip the introduction.

"'I confess,' said Brooks, 'that I killed the old man, but I did not murder him. I was trying to keep him from killing me. I had gone into a losing speculation and was in pressing need of money. I knew that it would be useless to ask him to help me; in fact, I didn't want him to know that I had been speculating, and I decided to help myself. I knew that he kept money in the safe at home; I didn't know how much, but I thought that it was enough to help me out, and I began deliberately to plan the robbery. I knew that it would have to be done in the moat skillful manner, for the old man's love of money made him as sharp as a briar when money was at stake; and I was resolved to have no confederates to share the reward and afterward to keep me in fear of exposure, I wrote a letter, and using the first name that came into my head, addressed it to "Dave Kittymunks, General Delivery, Chicago." I don't know where I picked up the name, and it makes no difference. I ran up to Milwaukee, dropped the letter in a mail box and was back here before any one knew that I was out of town. I disguised myself with black whiskers, went to the post-office and called for the letter, and took care that the delivery clerk should notice me. Colton supposed that none but members of his family knew of the safe at home, and why a robber should know must be made clear; so, wearing the same disguise, I called at the house one day and told the servant in charge that I had been sent to search for sewer-gas. I showed an order. A shrewd colored man had been discharged on account of some irregularities into which I had entrapped him, and an ignorant fellow that had agreed to work for less had just been put in his place. One evening when our family visited the Witherspoons I perfected my arrangements. I sawed the iron bars at the window and placed the black coat, with the Kittymunks letter in the pocket, as if the sash had failed and caught it. It was necessary that the coat should be found, and it was hardly natural that it should be found lying in the yard, it must appear that in his haste to get away the robber was compelled to leave his coat, and this could not be done unless he was forced to get out of it, leaving the police to suspect that he had done so with a struggle. I had torn one sleeve nearly off. But the mere falling of the sash on the tail of the coat would not do, it would pull out too easily. Then I thought of the pipe. I arranged the safe so that with a chisel I could open it easily—it was an old and insecure thing, anyway—and then placed a ladder on the ground under the window. Here there is a paved walk, so there was no necessity to make tracks. Now, there was but one thing more, and that was a noise to sound like the falling of the sash, and which was to wake the old man so that he might jump up almost in time to catch the robber. I had almost forgotten this, and now it puzzled me. The vault-room, a narrow apartment, is between the old man's room and mine, and I could have left the window up, propped with a stick, and from my window jerked out the prop, but the cool air would have shown the old man that the window was raised, and this would have ruined everything. Finally I decided that the falling of my own window—both are old-fashioned and are held up by a notched button—would arouse him and that he would think that the noise came from the vault-room. I would prop it with the edge of the button so that a slight pull on a string would throw it. But another question then arose. The weather was cold, and why should we have our window up so high? How should I explain to my wife? I would build a roaring fire in the furnace. That would heat the room too hot and give me an excuse to raise the window. But she would find it down. I could tell her that the room cooled off and that I put it down. But I was quibbling with myself. Everything was settled. The hall-door of the vault-room is but a step from my own door, and was kept fastened with a spring lock and a bolt and was supposed never to be opened. I drew back the bolt and the catch, and fixed the catch so that I could easily spring it when I went out. When everything had thus been arranged, I went to Witherspoon's to come home with the folks. The sky was clouded and the night was very dark. When we reached home the old man complained of having eaten too much—something he never had cause to complain of when he ate at home—and said that he believed he would lie down.

"'The window of the vault-room was never raised by the old man, and was kept fastened down with an old-time cast-iron catch. I had broken this off; but, afraid that he might examine the window and the door, I went with him to his room. And when he went into the vault-room to light the gas, I stood in the door and talked to him about his intended investment, and I talked so positively of the great profit he would surely make that he looked at neither the door nor the window. Everything had worked well. I bade him and the old lady good night and went to my own room. My wife complained of the heat, and I raised the window, remarking that I would get up after a while and put it down. How dreadfully slow the time was after I went to bed! And when I thought that every one must be asleep, my wife startled me by asking if I had noticed how unusually feeble her mother looked. I imagined that some one was dragging the ladder from under the window, and once I fancied that I heard the old man call me. The thought, the possibility of committing murder never occurred to me. The positive knowledge that I should never be discovered and that I should get every dollar of his money would not have tempted me to kill him. I lay for a long time—until I knew that every one must be asleep. Then I carefully got out of bed. I struck a chair, and I waited to see if my wife had been awakened by the noise. No; she was sound asleep. I tied a string to the window button, got my tools, which I had hidden in a closet and which were mainly intended for show after the robbery was discovered, and softly stole out. The hall was dark. The old man hated a gas-bill. I felt my way to the vault-room door and gently pushed it open, a little at a time. When I got inside I remembered that the very first thing I must attend to during the excitement which would follow the discovery of the robbery was to slip the bolt back in its place. The gas appeared to be burning lower than usual, and I wondered if the prospect of parting with money enough to make the investment had driven the old man to one more turn of his screw of economy. Although I knew how to open the safe, for previous arrangement had made it easy, I found it to be some trouble after all. But I got it open and had taken out the money drawer when a noise startled me. I sprang up, and there was the old man. He was but a few feet from me. He had a pistol. I saw it gleam in the dim light. I couldn't stand discovery, and I must protect myself against being shot. I knew that in the semi-darkness he did not recognize me. All this came with a flash. I sprang upon him. With one hand I caught the pistol, with the other I clutched his throat. I would choke him senseless and run back to my room. He threw up one hand, threw back his head and freed his throat. We were under the gas jet. My hand struck the screw, and the light leaped to full blaze. At that instant the pistol fired and the old man fell, I wheeled about and was in the hall; I sprung the lock after me, and in a second I was in my own room—just as my wife, dazed with fright, had jumped out of bed. "Come," I cried, "something must have happened." And together we ran into the old man's room.'"

"'During the excitement which followed I forgot no precaution; I slipped the bolt back into place and removed the string from the button of my own window. My wife was frantic. I did not suspect that the old woman had seen me, for I was not in the vault-room an instant after the pistol fired, and before that it was so dark that she could not have recognized me. If I had thought that she did see me'—"

"'What would you have done?' the reporter asked."

"'I don't know,' Brooks answered, 'but it is not reasonable to suppose that I would have let her go away from home. I acknowledge that I did not care to see her recover—now that I am acknowledging everything—for at best she could be only in the way, and naturally, she would interfere with my management of the estate. But if I had been anxious that she should die, I could have had her poisoned. Instead, however, I employed a quack, who I knew pretended to be a great physician, and who I believed could do her no good. In fact, I didn't think that she could live but a few days.' After pausing for a moment he added, 'She must have seen me just as the light blazed up, and was doubtless standing back from the door. I didn't take any money.'"

"'But why didn't you take the money while the old man was away? Then you would have run no risk of killing him or of being killed."

"'I could easily have done this, but he was so shrewd. I wanted him to believe that he had almost caught the robber.'"

"'Then there is no such man as Dave Kittymunks,' said the reporter."

"'No,' Brooks answered."

"'But Flummers, the reporter, said that he knew him.'"

"'I met Mr. Flummers one evening,' Brooks replied, 'and before we parted company I think that he must have had in his mind a vague recollection of having seen such a fellow. The public was eager, and that was a great stimulus to Mr. Flummers.'"

"'Did you feel that you were suspected?' the reporter asked."

"'Not of having committed the murder, but I felt that I was suspected of having had something to do with it. But I hadn't a suspicion that any proof existed. I could stand suspicion, especially as I should receive large pay for it. A number of men in this city are under suspicion of one kind or another, but it doesn't seem to have hurt them a great deal. Their checks are good. Men come back from the penitentiary and build up fortunes with the money they stole. Their hammered brass fronts and colored electric lights are not unknown to Clark Street.'"

"'But you suffered remorse, of course,' the reporter suggested."

"'I think that there is a great deal of humbug about the remorse a man feels,' Brooks replied. 'I regretted that I had been forced to kill the old man, for with all his stinginess he was rather kind-hearted, but I had to save my own life. It is true that I didn't have to commit the robbery, but robbery is not a capital crime.'"

"'But the self-defense of a robber, when it results in a tragedy, is a murder,' the reporter suggested."

"'We'll see about that,' Brooks coolishly replied."

"'Do you make this confession with the advice of your lawyer?'"

"'No, but at the suggestion of my own judgment. When I was told that the old woman had seen the killing and that, of course, her deposition would be introduced in court, I then knew that it was worse than useless to protest my innocence. Besides, as she saw it, the tragedy was a murder, but, as I confess it'—He hesitated."

"'It is what?' the reporter asked."

"'Well, that's for the law to determine. There should always be some mercy for a man who tells the truth. I have done a desperate thing—I staked my future on it. But I have associated with rich men so long that for me a future without money could be but a continuation of embarrassment. I have helped to make the fortunes of other men, but I failed when I engaged in speculations for myself. I had prospects, it is true, but I didn't know but Colton had arranged his will so as to prevent my using his money; and I had reason to fear that my wife was in touch with him,'"

"'Has she been to see you?' the reporter asked."

"'That's rather an impertinent question,' Brooks replied, 'but I may as well confess everything. We haven't been getting along very well together. No, she hasn't been to see me. Not one of my friends has called. There, gentlemen, I have told you everything.'"

When the last word of the interview had been pronounced, Witherspoon grunted and lay back with his hands clasped under his head.

"What do you think of it?" Henry asked.

"There's hardly any room for thinking."

But he did think, and a few moments later he said: "Of all the cold-blooded scoundrels I ever heard of, he takes the lead. And just to think what I have done for him! I don't think, though, that he has robbed us of much. He didn't have the handling of a great deal of cash. Still I can't tell. My, how sharp he is! He didn't mention the Colossus. But what difference Would it make?" He sat up. "What need I care how often he mentions it? The public knows me. Nobody ever had cause to question my credit. Why should I have been worried over him? Henry, you are right; my trouble is the result of a physical cause. Caroline, I'm going in to dinner with you."

Opie Read

CHAPTER XXVII

POINTS OUT HER BROTHER'S DUTY

In the afternoon of the day that followed the publication of the confession Flummers minced his way into the Press Club. He wore a suit of new clothes, and although the weather was warm, he carried a silk-faced overcoat. Before any one took notice of him he put his coat and hat on the piano, and then, with a gesture, he exclaimed:

"*Wow!*"

"Why, here's Kittymunks! Helloa, Kit!" one man shouted. "Have you identified Brooks?" some one else cried, and a roar followed.

For a moment Flummers stood smiling at this raillery; then suddenly, and as though he would shut out a humiliating scene, he pressed his hands across his eyes. But his hands flew off into a double gesture—into a gathering motion that invited every one to come into his confidence, and solemnly he pronounced these words:

"He made a monkey of me."

"I should say he did!" Whittlesy cried. "Oh, you'll hold me in the hollow of your hand, will you?"

Flummers looked at Whittlesy and scalloped the forerunner of a withering speech; but, thoughtful enough suddenly to remember that at this solemn time his words and his eyes belonged not to one man, but to the entire company, he withdrew his gaze from Whittlesy, and in his broad look included every one present.

"He made a monkey of me. He stopped me on the street one evening—I had boned him for an advertisement when I was running *The Art of Interior Decoration*—and was so polite that I said to myself: 'Papa, here's another flip man thirsting for recognition. Put him on your staff.' Well, we had a bowl or two at Garry's, and the first thing I knew he began to remind me that I remembered a fellow who must be Kittymunks, and I said, 'Hi, gi, here's a scoop.' And it was. Oh, it's a pretty hard matter to scoop papa"—(tapping his head). "Papa knows what the public wants, and he serves it up. Some of you dry-dock conservative ducks would have let it go by, but papa is nothing if not adventurous. Papa knows that without adventure you make no discoveries. But, wow! he did make a monkey of me. Just think of a floor-walker making a monkey of papa!" He pressed his hand to his brow. "Why, a floor-walker has been my especial delicacy—he has been my appetizer, my white-meat—but, wow! this fellow was a gristle."

"Mr. Flummers," said McGlenn, "we all love you."

"Say, John, I owe you two dollars."

"No, Mr. Flummers, you don't owe me anything."

"But I borrowed two dollars from you, John, when I started *The Bankers' Review.*"

Opie Read

"No man can borrow money from me, Mr. Flummers. If he gets money from me, it's his and not mine. We all love you, Mr. Flummers, and your Kittymunks escapade, so thoroughly in keeping with our estimate of you, has added strength to our affection. If you wish to keep friends, Mr. Flummers, you must do nothing which they could not forecast for you. The development of hitherto undiscovered traits, of an unsuspected and therefore an inconsistent strength, is a dash of cold water in the face of friendship. We are tied to you by a strong rope made of the strands of weaknesses, Mr. Flummers."

"Oh, no."

"Yes, made of the fine-spun strands of weaknesses, Mr. Flummers. It is better to be a joss of pleasing indiscretion than to be a man of great strength, for the joss has no enemies, but sooner or later the strong man must be overthrown by the hoard of weaklings that envy has set against him. Do you desire something to drink, Mr. Flummers?"

"No."

"Now you place your feet on inconsistent and slippery ground, Mr. Flummers. Remember that in order to hold our love you must not surprise us."

"But I can't drink now; I have just had something to eat."

"Beware, Mr. Flummers. Inconsiderate eating caused a great general to lose a battle, and now you are in danger. You may suffer superfluous lunch to change our opinion of you, which means a withdrawal of our love."

"Oh, wait a minute or two, John. But never mind. Say, there, boy, bring me a little liquor. But, say, wasn't it funny that

Detective Stavers should give ten thousand dollars of that reward to the Home for the Friendless? I used to work for the Pinkertons, and I know all those guys, and there's not one of the whole gang that gives a snap for charity. There's a mystery about it somewhere."

"Probably you can throw some light on it as you did on the Kittymunks affair," Whittlesy suggested.

Flummers gave him a scallop. "Papa still holds you in the hollow of his hand. Here you are; see?" He put his finger in the palm of his hand. "You are right there; see? And when I want you, I'm going to shut down, this way." He closed his hand. "And people will wonder what papa's carrying around with him, but you'll know all the time."

"My," said Whittlesy, "what a dangerous man this fellow would be if he had nerve! Oh, yes, people will wonder what you have in the hollow of your hand, and sooner or later, they will find that you are carrying three shells and a pea. Get out, Kittymunks. I'm afraid of you—too tough for me."

Flummers waved Whittlesy into oblivion, and continued: "Old Witherspoon gave up his check for twenty thousand, and there the reward stops, for Mrs. Brooks won't give anything for having her husband caught. It has been whispered in the *Star* office that Henry Witherspoon had something to do with the detection of Brooks, and made Stavers promise that he would give half the reward to charity. But I don't believe it. Why should he want to give up ten thousand? But there's a mystery in it somewhere, and the first thing you know papa'll get on the track of it. Here, boy, bring that drink. What have you been doing out there? Have I got to drink alone? Well, I'm equal to any emergency." He shuddered as he swallowed the whisky, but recovered instantly, and with a circular movement, expressive of his satisfaction, rubbed his growing paunch.

Witherspoon remained three days at home and then resumed his place at the store. With a promptness in which he took a pride, he sent a check to the detective. He did this even before he went down to the Colossus. The physician had urged him to put aside all business cares, and the merchant had replied with a contemptuous grunt. He appeared to be stronger when he came home at evening, and he joked with Ellen; he told her that she had narrowly escaped the position of temporary manager of the Colossus. They were in the library, and a cheerfulness that had been absent seemed just to have returned. Witherspoon went early to bed and left Henry and Ellen sitting there.

"Don't you think he will be well in a few days?" the girl asked.

"Yes, now that his worry is locked in jail."

"That isn't so very bad," she replied, smiling at him. "But suppose they hang his worry?"

"It may be all the better."

"Mother and I went this afternoon to see Mrs. Brooks," said the girl. "And she doesn't appear to be crushed, either. I don't see why she should be—they wouldn't have lived together much longer anyway. Oh, of course she's humiliated and all that, but if she really cared for him she'd be heartbroken. She used to tell me how handsome he was, but that was before they were married. I think she must have found out lately what she might have known at first—that he married her for money. Oh, she's a good woman—there's no doubt of that— but she's surely as plain a creature as I've ever seen."

"If I had thought that she loved him," said Henry, "I should have hesitated a long time before seeking to fasten the murder on him. I may have only a vague regard for justice, for abstract right is so intangible; but I have a strong and definite sympathy."

"We all have," she said. "Oh, by the way," she broke off, as though by mere accident she had thought of something, "you superintended the Colossus for two whole days, didn't you?"

"I didn't exactly superintend it, but I stood about with an air of helpless authority."

"But how did you get along with your paper during all that worry?" she asked; and before he answered she added, "I don't see how you could write anything."

"Worry is a bad producer, but a good critic," Henry replied. "And I didn't try to write much," he added.

She put her elbows on the arm of her chair, rested her chin on her hand and leaned toward him. "Do you know what I've been thinking of ever since I came home?" she asked.

"Well," he answered, smiling on her, "as you haven't told me and as I am not a mind-reader, I can't say that I do."

"Must I tell you?"

"Yes."

"And you won't be put out?"

"Surely not. You wouldn't want to tell me if you thought it would put me out, would you?"

"No, but I was afraid this might." She hesitated. "I have been thinking that you ought to go into business with father. Wait a moment, now, please. You said you wouldn't be put out. You see how much he needs you, and you ought to be willing to make a personal sacrifice. You"—

He reached over and put his hand on her head. She looked into his eyes. "Ellen, there is but one thing that binds me to a past that was a hardship, but which after all was a liberty; and that one thing is the fact that I am independent of the Colossus, the mill where thousands of feet are treading. I have one glimpse of freedom, and that is through the window of my office. It isn't possible that you can wholly understand me, but let me tell you one time for all that I shall have nothing to do with the store."

She put his hand off her head and settled back in her chair. "I thought you might if I asked you, but I ought to have known that nothing I could say would have any effect. You don't care for me; you don't care for any of us."

"Ellen, it is but natural that you should side with father against me, and it is also natural that I should decide in favor of myself. You may say that on my part it is selfishness, and I may say that it is more just than selfish. But you must *not* say that I don't care for you."

"Oh, it is easy enough for you to say that you *do* care for me," she replied. "It costs but a breath that must be breathed anyway; but if you really cared for me you would do as I ask you—as I beg of you."

"Well," and he laughed at her, "there is a charming narrowness in that view, I must say. If I love you I will grant whatever you may ask; and if you love me—then what? Shall I answer?"

"Yes," she said, "as you seem to know what answer will be most acceptable to you."

"No, not the answer most acceptable to me, but the one that seems to be the most consistent. And if you love me," he continued, in answer to the question, "you will not ask me to make a painful sacrifice." He looked earnestly at her and added: "I think you'd better call me a crank and dismiss the subject."

He expected her to take this as a humorous smoothing of their first unpleasant ruffle, but if she did she shrewdly deceived him, for she looked at him with the soberest of inquiry as she asked:

"Do you really think you are a crank?"

"I sometimes think so," he answered.

"Isn't it simply that you take a pride in being different from other people. Don't you strive to be odd?"

"Are you talking seriously?" he asked.

"Yes."

"Well, then, I will say seriously that I do take a pride in being different from some people?"

"Am I included?"

"Oh, nonsense, girl. What are you thinking about?"

"Oh, I know you don't care for any of us," she whimpered. "You won't even let mother show her love for you; you try to surround yourself with a lordly mystery."

"If I have a mystery it is far from a lordly one."

"But it's not far from annoying, I can tell you that."

"Don't try to pick a quarrel, little girl."

"Oh, I'm not half so anxious to quarrel as you are."

"All right; if that's the case, we'll get along smoothly. Get your doll out of the little trunk and let us play with her."

She got up and stood with her hands resting on the back of the chair. "If I didn't have to like you, Henry, I wouldn't like you a single bit. But somehow I can't help it. It must be because I can't understand you."

"Then why do you blame me for not making myself plain, since your regard depends upon the uncertain light in which you see me?"

"You are so funny," she said.

"Then you ought to laugh at me instead of scolding."

"Indeed! But if I didn't scold sometimes you would rim over me; and besides, we shouldn't have the happiness that comes from making up again. Really, though, won't you think about what I have said?"

"I will think about you, and that will include all that you have said and all that you may say."

"I oughtn't to kiss you good night, but after that I suppose I must. There—Mr.—Ungratefulness. Good night."

CHAPTER XXVIII

THE VERDICT

During the first few weeks of his imprisonment, the murderer of old man Colton had maintained a lightsome air, but as the time for his trial drew near he appeared to lose the command of that self-hypnotism which had seemed to extract gayety from wretchedness. To one who has been condemned to death there comes a resignation that is deeper than a philosophy. Despair has killed the nerve that fear exposed, and nothing is left for terror to feed on. But Brooks had not this deadened resignation, for he had a hope that he might escape the gallows, and so long as there is a hope there is an anxiety. He had refused to see his wife, for he felt that in her heart she had condemned him and executed the sentence; but he was anxious to see Witherspoon. He thought that with the aid of that logic which trade teaches and which in its directness comes near being an intellectual grace, he could explain himself to the merchant and thereby whiten his crime, and he sent for him; but the messenger returned with a note that bore words which Brooks had often heard Witherspoon speak and which he himself so often had repeated: "Explain to the law."

The trial came. In the expectancy with which Chicago looks for a new sensation, Brooks had been almost forgotten by the public. His confession had robbed his trial of that uncertainty which means excitement, and there now remained but a formal ceremony, the appointment of his time to die. The newspapers no longer paid especial attention to him, and such neglect depresses a murderer, for notoriety is his last intoxicant. It seemed that an unwarranted length of time was taken up in the selection of a jury, a deliberation that usually exposes justice to many dangers; and after this the trial proceeded. The deposition of Mrs. Colton was introduced. It was a brief statement, and after leading up to the vital point, thus concluded: "I must have been asleep some time, when my husband awoke me. He said that he thought he heard a noise in the vault-room. I listened for a few moments and replied that I didn't think it was anything. But he got up and took his pistol from under the pillow and went into the vault-room. A moment later I was convinced that I heard something, and I got up, and just as I got near the door the light blazed up and at the same moment there was a loud report as of a pistol; and then I saw my husband fall—saw Mr. Brooks wheel about and run out of the room. This is all I remember until I found myself lying on the bed, unable to move or speak."

Brooks set up a plea for mercy, and his lawyers were strong in the urging of it, but when the judge delivered his charge it was clear that the plea was not entertained by the court. The jury retired, and now the courtroom was thronged. To idle men there is a fascination in the expected verdict, even though it may not admit of the quality of speculation. The jurymen could not be out long—their duty was well defined; but an hour passed, and the crowd began gradually to melt away. Two hours—and word came that the jury could not agree. It was now dark, and the court was adjourned to meet in evening session. But midnight struck, and still there was no verdict. What could be the cause of this indecision? It was a mystery outside, but within the room it was plain. One man had hung the jury. In his community he was so well known as a sectarian that he was called a hypocrite. He was not thought to be strong except in the grasp he held upon bigotry, but he succeeded in either convincing or brow-beating eleven men into an agreement not to hang Brooks, but to send him to the penitentiary for life; and this verdict was rendered when the court reassembled at morning.

Witherspoon was sitting in his office at the Colossus when Henry entered. Papers were piled upon the merchant's desk, but he regarded them not. A boy stood near as if waiting for orders, but Witherspoon took no heed of him. He sat in a reverie, and as Henry entered he started as if rudely aroused from sleep.

"Have you heard the verdict?" Henry asked.

"By telephone," Witherspoon answered. "Sit down."

"No, I must get over to the office. What do you think of the verdict?"

"If the law's satisfied I am," Witherspoon answered. "But you wanted him hanged, didn't you?" he added.

"No, but I wanted him punished. The truth is, I hated the fellow almost from the first."

Witherspoon turned to the boy and asked: "What do you want? Oh, did I ring for you? Well, you may go." And then he spoke to Henry: "You hated him."

"Yes."

"Why?"

"Because he is a villain."

"But if you hated him from the first, you hated him before you found out that he was a villain; and that was snap judgment. I try a man before I condemn him."

"And I let a man condemn himself, and some men do this the minute I see them."

"But a quick judgment is nearly always wrong."

"Yes, and yet it's better than a slow judgment that allows itself to be imposed upon."

"Sometimes," Witherspoon agreed; and after a short silence he added: "I was just thinking of how that fellow imposed on me, but I can't quite get at the cause of my worry over him, and I don't understand why I should have been afraid that he could ruin me. I want to ask you something, and I want you to tell me the exact truth without fear of giving offense: Have you ever thought that at times my mind was unbalanced? Have you?"

"You haven't been well, and a sick man's mind is never sound, you know."

"That's all true enough; but do I remind you very much of your uncle Andrew?"

"Yes, when you worry."

"I thought so. I've got to stop worrying; and I believe that we have more control over ourselves than we exercise. Come back at noon and we'll go out together."

"I'll be here," Henry replied.

Just before he reached the office Henry met John Richmond, and together they stepped into a cigar-store.

"I've been over to your office," said Richmond. "I have important business with you."

"All right, John. Business with you is a pleasure."

"I think this will be. This is the last day of September, and relying on my recollection, I know that black bass are about ready to begin their fall campaign. So I thought we'd better get on a train early to-morrow morning and go out into Lake County. Now don't say you are too busy, for *I'm* running away from a stack of work as high as my head."

"I'll go."

"Good. We'll have a glorious day in the woods. We'll forget Brother Brooks and the fanatic who saved his life; we'll float on the lake; well pick up nuts; we'll listen to the controversy of the blue jays, and the flicker, flicker of the yellow-hammers; we'll study Mr. Woodpecker, whose judgment tells him to go south, but who is held back by the promising sunshine. The train leaves at eight. I'll be on hand, and don't you fail."

"I won't. I'm only too anxious to get out of town."

Shortly after Henry arrived at the office Miss Drury came into his room. "Your sister was here just now," she said.

"Was she?"

"Yes, she came to wait for the verdict."

"That reminds me. I intended to telephone, but forgot it."

"She said she knew you wouldn't think of it."

"Did you quarrel?" Henry asked.

"Did we quarrel? Well, now, I like that question. No, we didn't quarrel. I got along with her quite as well as I do with her brother. She said that she had often wondered who got up my department, but that no one had ever told her."

"She may have wondered, but she never asked. So, you see, I intend to rid myself of blame even at the expense of my sister."

"Oh, I suppose she said it merely to put me in good humor with myself."

"But wouldn't it have been more in harmony with a woman's character if she'd given you a sly cut, a tiny stab, to put you in ill humor with the world?"

"I hope you don't mean that, Mr. Witherspoon."

"Why? Would it make you think less of women?"

"What egotism! No, less of you."

"Oh, if that's the case I'll withdraw it—will say that I didn't mean it."

"That's so kind of you that I'm almost glad you said it."

She went back to her work, but a few moments later she returned, and now she appeared to be embarrassed. "You must pardon me," she said.

"Pardon you? What for?"

"For speaking so rudely just now. You constantly make me forget that I am working for you."

"That's a high compliment. But I didn't notice that you spoke rudely."

"Yes, I said 'what egotism,' and I'm sorry."

"You must not be sorry, for if you meant what you said, I deserved it."

"Oh, then you really did mean what you said about women."

Henry laughed. "Miss Drury, don't worry over anything I say; and remember that I'm pleased whenever you forget that you are working for me. You didn't know that I was instrumental in the arrest of Brooks, did you?"

"Why, no, I never thought of such a thing."

"You must keep it to yourself, but I was, and why? I hated him. Once he suggested to me that he would like to have you take lunch with him. I told him that you didn't go out with any one, and with coldbloodedness he replied, 'Ah, she hasn't been here long.' I hated him from that moment. Don't you see what a narrow-minded fellow I am?"

"Narrow-minded!"

"Yes, to move the law against a man merely because he had spoken lightly of—of my friend."

She was leaning against the door-case and was looking down. She dropped a paper. Henry glanced at the window, which he called his loop-hole of freedom, for through it no

Colossus could be seen. He turned slowly and looked toward the door. The girl was gone.

CHAPTER XXIX

A DAY OF REST

Early the next morning Henry and Richmond were on a train, speeding away from the roar, the clang, the turmoil, the smoke, the atmospheric streams of stench, the trouble of the city. They saw a funeral procession, and Richmond remarked: "They have killed a drone and are dragging him out of the hive, and as they have set out so early they must be going to pay him the compliment of a long haul." They passed stations where men who had spent a quiet night at home paced up and down impatiently waiting for a train to whirl them back to their daily strife. "They play cards going in and coming out," said Richmond, "but at noon they are eager to cut one another's throats."

They ran through a forest, dense and wild-looking, but in the wildness there was a touch of man's deceiving art. They crossed a small river and caught sight of a barefooted boy trying to steal a boat. They sped over the prairie and flew past an old Dutch windmill. It was an odd sight, an un-American glimpse—a wink at a strange land. They commented on everything that whirled within sight—a bend in the road, a crooked Line, a tumble-down fence. They were boys. They talked about names that they held a prejudice against, and occasionally one of them would say, "No, I don't like a man of that name."

"There," Richmond spoke up, "I never knew a man of that name that wasn't a wolf. But sometimes one good fellow offsets a whole generation of bad names. I never liked the name Witherspoon until I met you."

"How do you like DeGolyer?" Henry asked.

"That's not so had, but it isn't free from political scandal. I rather like it—strikes me that there might be a pretty good fellow of that name. Let me see. We'll get off about three miles this side of Lake Villa and go over to Fourth Lake. The woods over there are beautiful."

"We should have insisted on McGlenn's coming," said Henry.

"No," Richmond replied, "the country is a bore to John. Once he came out with me and found fault with what he termed the loose methods of nature. I pointed out a hill, and he said that it wasn't so graceful as a mound in the park. I waved my hand toward a pastoral stretch of valley, and he said, 'Yes, but it isn't Drexel Boulevard.' Art is the mistress of John's mind. His emotions are never stirred by a simple tune, but the climax of an opera tumbles him over and over in ecstasy. He is one of the truest of friends, and he is as game as a brook trout. He has associated with drunkards, but was never drunk; and during his early days in Chicago he lived with gamblers, but he came out an honorable man."

"I have been reading his novels," said Henry, "and in places he is as sharp as broken glass."

"Yes, but he is too much given to didacticism. Out of mischief I tell him that he sets up a theory, calls it a character, and talks through it. But he is strong, and his technique is fine."

"In Paris he would have been a great man," Henry replied.

They got off at a milk station and strolled along a road. A piece of newspaper fluttered on the ground in front of them.

"There is just enough of a breeze to stir a scandal," said Richmond, treading upon the paper.

"When I find a newspaper in an out-of-the-way place," Henry replied, "I fancy that the world has lost one of its visiting-cards."

They stopped at a farm-house, engaged a boat, and then went down to the lake. Nature wore a thoughtful, contemplative smile, and the lake was a dimple. A flawless day; an Indian summer day, gauzed with a glowing haze. And the smaller trees, in recognition of this grape-juice time of year, had adorned themselves in red. October, the sweetest and mellowest stanza in God Almighty's poem—the dreamy, lulling lines between hot Summer's passion and Winter's cold severity. On the train they had been boys, but now they were men, looking at the tranquil, listening to the immortal.

"Did you speak?" Henry asked.

"No," said Richmond, "it was October."

They floated out on the lake. Mud-hens, in their midsummer fluttering, had woven the rushes into a Gobelin tapestry. The deep notes of the old frog were hushed, but in an out-of-the-way nook the youngster was trying his voice on the water-dog. A dragon-fly lighted on a stake and flashed a sunbeam from his bedazzled wing; and a bright bug, like a streak of blue flame, zigzagged his way across the smooth water.

An hour passed. "They won't bite," said Richmond. "In this pervading dreaminess they have forgotten their materialism."

"Probably they are tired of minnows," Henry replied. "Suppose we try frogs."

"No, I have sworn never to bait with another frog. It's too much like patting a human being on a hook. The last frog I used reached up, took hold of the hook and tried to take it out. No, I can't fish with a frog."

"But you would catch a bass, and you know that it must hurt him—in fact, you know that it's generally fatal."

"Yes, but it's his rapacity that gets him into trouble. I don't believe they're going to bite. Suppose we go over yonder and wallow under that tree."

"All right. I don't care to catch a fish now anyway. It would be a disturbance to pull him out. Our trip has already paid us a large profit. With one exception it has been more than a year since I have seen anything outside of that monstrous town. As long as the spirit of the child remains with the man, he loves the country. All children are fond of the woods—the deep shade holds a mystery."

They lay on the thick grass under an oak. On one side of the tree was an old scar, made with an axe, and Henry, pointing to the scar, said: "To cut down this tree was once the task assigned some lusty young fellow, but just as he had begun his work, a neighbor came along and told him that his strong arm was needed by his country; and he put down his axe and took up a gun."

"That may be," Richmond replied, "Many a hero has sprung from this land; these meadows have many times been mowed by men who went away to reap and who were reaped at Gettysburg."

After a time they went out in the boat again, and were on the water when the sun lost its splendor and, hanging low, fired the distant wood-top. And now there was a hush as if all the universe waited for the dozing day to sink into sounder sleep. The sun went down, a bird screamed, and nature began her evening hum.

In the darkness they lost the path that led through the woods. They made an adventure of this, and pretended that they might not find their way out until morning. They wandered about in a laughing aimlessness, and there was a tone of disappointment in Richmond's voice when he halted and said, "Here's the road."

They went to bed in the farmer's spare room, where the subscription book, flashing without and dull within, lay on the center table. A plaster-of-paris kitten, once the idol of a child whose son now doubtless lay in a national burial-ground, looked down from the mantel-piece. There was the frail rocking-chair that was never intended to be sat in, and on the wall, in an acorn-studded frame, was a faded picture entitled "The Return of the Prodigal."

Richmond was sinking to sleep when Henry called him.

"What is it?"

"I didn't know you were asleep."

"I wasn't. What were you going to say?"

"Oh, nothing in particular—was just going to ask what you think of a man who lives a lie?"

"I should think," Richmond answered, "that he must be a pretty natural sort of a fellow."

CHAPTER XXX

A MOTHER'S REQUEST

At dinner, the evening after Henry had returned from the country, Ellen caused her mother to look up by saying that Miss Miller's chance was gone.

"What do you mean?" Mrs. Witherspoon asked. "I wasn't aware that Miss Miller ever had any chance, as you are pleased to term it. But why hasn't she as much chance now as she ever had?"

"Because her opportunity has been killed."

"Was it ever alive?" Henry asked.

"Oh, yes, but it is dead now. Mother, you ought to see the young woman I saw at Henry's office the other day. Look, he's trying to blush. Oh, she's dazzling with her great blue eyes."

Mrs. Witherspoon's look demanded an explanation.

"Mother," said Henry, "she means our book-reviewer."

"I don't like literary women," Mrs. Witherspoon replied, with

Opie Read

stress in the movement of her head and with prejudice in the compression of her lips. "They are too—too uppish, I may say."

"But Miss Drury makes no literary pretensions," Henry rejoined.

"I should think not," Ellen spoke up. "I didn't take her to be literary, she was so neatly dressed."

"When you cease so lightly to discuss a noble-minded girl—a friend of mine—you will do me a great favor," Henry replied.

"What's all this?" Witherspoon asked. He had paid no attention to this trifling set-to and had caught merely the last accent of it.

"Oh, nothing, I'm sure," Ellen answered.

"Very well, then, we can easily put it aside. Henry, what was it you said to-day at noon about going away?"

"I said that I was going with a newspaper excursion to Mexico."

"Oh, surely, not so far as that!" Mrs. Witherspoon exclaimed.

"It won't take long, mother."

"No, but it's so far; and I should think that you've had enough of that country."

"I've never been in Mexico."

"Oh, well, all those countries down there are just the same, and I should think that when you have seen one your first impression is that you don't want to see another."

"They are restful at any rate," he replied.

"But can't you rest nearer home?"

"I could, but I have made up my mind to go with this excursion. I'll not be gone long."

"When are you going to start?"

"To-morrow evening."

"So soon as that?"

"Yes; I—I didn't decide until to-day."

"I don't like to have you go so far, but you know best, I suppose. Are you going out this evening?" she asked.

"No."

"Well, I wish to have a talk with you alone. Come to my sitting-room."

"With pleasure," he answered.

He thought that he knew the subject upon which she had chosen to talk; he saw that she was worried over Miss Drury; but when he had gone into her room and taken a seat beside her, he was surprised that she began to speak of Witherspoon's health.

"I know," she said, "that he is getting stronger, but he needs one great stimulus—he needs you. Please don't look at me that way." She took his hand, and it was limp in her warm grasp. "You know that I've always taken your part."

"Yes, mother, God bless you."

"And you know that I wouldn't advise you against your own interest—you know, my son, that I love you."

His hand closed upon hers, and his eyes, which for a moment had been cold and rebellious, now were warm with the light of affection and obedience.

"I will do what you ask," he said.

"God bless you, my son."

She arose, and hastening to the door, called: "George! oh, George!"

Witherspoon answered, and a moment later he came into the room. "George, our son will take his proper place."

Henry got up, and the merchant caught him by the hand. "You don't know how strong this makes me!" He rubbed his eyes and continued: "This is the first time I have seen you in your true light. You are a strong man—you are not easily influenced. Sit down; I want to look at you. Yes, you are a strong man, and you will be stronger. I will buy the Colton interest—the Witherspoons shall be known everywhere. To-morrow we will make the arrangements."

"I start for Mexico to-morrow."

"Yes, but you'll not be gone long. The trip will be good for you. Let me have a chair," he said. "Thank you," he added, when a chair had been placed for him. "I am quite beside myself—I see things in a new light." He sat down, reached over and took Henry's hands; he shoved himself back and looked at the young man. "Age is coming on, but I'll see myself reproduced."

"But not supplanted," Henry said.

"No, not until the time comes. But the time must come. Ah, after this life, what then? To be remembered. But what serves this purpose? A perpetuation of our interests. After you, your son—the man dies, but the name lives. No one of any sensibility can look calmly on the extinction of his name."

He arose with a new ease, and with a vigor that had long been absent from his step, paced up and down the room. "You will not find it a sacrifice, my son; it will become a fascination. It is not the love of money, but the conscious-ness of force. The lion enjoys his own strength, but the hare is frightened at his own weakness and runs when no danger is near. Small tradesmen may be ignorant, but a large merchant must be wise, for his wisdom has made him large. Trade is the realization of logic, and success is the fruit of philosophy. People wonder at the achievements of a man whom they take to be ignorant; but that man has a secret intelligence somewhere; and if they could discover it they would imitate him. Don't you permit yourself to feel that any mental force is too high for business. The statesman is but a business man. Behind the great general is the nation's backbone, and that backbone is a financier. Let me see, what time is it?" He looked at his watch. "Come, we will all go to the theater."

Witherspoon drove Henry to the railway station the next evening, and during the drive he talked almost ceaselessly. He complimented Henry upon the wise slowness with which he had made up his mind; there was always too much of impulse in a quick decision. He pointed his whip at a house and said: "A lonely old man lives there; he has built up a fortune, but his name will be buried with him." He spoke of his religious views. There must be a hereafter, but in the future state strength must rule; it was the order of the universe, the will of nature, the decree of eternity. He talked of the books that he had read, and then he turned to business. In a commercial transaction there must be no sentiment; financial credit must be guarded as a sacred honor. Every debt must be paid; every cent due must be extracted. It might cause distress, but distress was an inheritance of life.

To this talk the young man listened vaguely; he said neither yes nor no, and his silence was taken for close attention.

When they arrived at the station, Witherspoon got out of the buggy and with Henry walked up and down the concrete floor along the iron fence. It was here that the stranger had wonderingly gazed at the crowd as he held up young Henry's chain.

"Are you going through New Orleans?"

"Yes; will be there one day."

"You are pretty well acquainted in that town, I suppose."

"With the streets," Henry answered.

"I wish I could go with you, but I can't. Next year perhaps I can get away oftener."

"Yes, if you have cause to place confidence in me."

"I have the confidence now; all that remains for you to do is to become acquainted with the details of your new position."

"And there the trouble may lie."

"You underrate yourself. A man who can pick up an education can with a teacher learn to do almost anything."

"But when I was a boy there was a pleasure in a lesson because I felt that I was stealing it."

The merchant laughed and drew Henry closer to him. "If we may believe the envious, the quality of theft may not be lacking in your future work," he said.

After a short silence Henry remarked: "You say that I am to perpetuate your name."

"Yes, surely."

"I suppose, then, that you claim the right to direct me in my selection of a wife."

Again the merchant drew Henry closer to him. "Not to direct, but to advise," he answered.

"A rich girl, I presume."

"A suitable match at least."

"Suitable to you or to me?"

"To both—to us all. But we'll think about that after a while."

"I have thought about it; the girl is penniless."

"What! I hope you haven't committed yourself." They were

farther apart now.

"Not by what I have uttered—and she may care nothing for me—but my actions must have said that I love her."

"What do you mean by 'love her'?" the merchant angrily demanded.

"Is it possible that you have forgotten?"

"Of course not," he said, softening. "Who is she?"

"A girl whose life has been a devotion—an angel."

"Bosh! That's all romance. Young man, this is Chicago, and Chicago is the material end—the culmination of the nineteenth century."

"And this girl is the culmination of purity and divine womanhood—of love!" He stopped short, looked at Witherspoon, and said: "If you say a word against her I will not go into the store—I'll set fire to it and burn it down."

They were in a far corner, and now, standing apart, were looking at each other. The young man's eyes snapped with anger.

"Come, don't fly off that way," said the merchant. "You may choose for yourself, of course. Oh, you've got some of the old man's pigheadedness, have you? All right; it will keep men from running over you."

He took Henry's arm, and they walked back toward the gate.

"I won't say anything to your mother about it."

"You may do as you like."

"Well, it's best not to mention it yet a while. Will you sell your newspaper as soon as you return?"

"Yes."

"All right. Then there'll be nothing in the way. Your train's about ready. Take good care of yourself, and come back rested. Telegraph me whenever you can. Good-by."

CHAPTER XXXI

A MOMENT OF ARROGANCE

Henry wandered through the old familiar streets. How vividly came back the years, the dreary long ago! Here, on a door-step, he had passed many a nodding hour, kept in half-consciousness by the clank of the printing-press, waiting for the dawn and his bundle of newspapers. No change had come to soften the truth of the picture that a by-gone wretchedness threw upon his memory. The attractive fades, but how eternal is the desolate! Yonder he could see the damp wall where he used to hunt for snails, and farther down the narrow street was the house in which had lived the old Italian woman. "You think I'm a stranger," he mused, as he passed a policeman, "but I know all this. I have been in dens here that you have never seen."

He went to the Foundlings' Home and walked up and down in front of the long, low building. An old woman, dragging a rocking-chair, came out on the veranda and sat down. He halted at the gate, stood for a moment and then rang the bell. A negro opened the gate and politely invited him to enter. The old woman arose as he came up the steps.

"Keep your seat, madam."

"Did you want to see anybody?" she asked.

"No; and don't let me disturb you."

He gave her a closer look and thought that he remembered her as the woman who had taken him on her lap and told him that his father was dead.

"No disturbance at all," she answered. "Is there anything I can do for you?"

"Yes, I should like to look through this place."

"Very well, but you may find things pretty badly tumbled up. We're cleaning house. Come this way, please."

He saw the corner in which he used to sleep, and there was the same iron bedstead, with a fever-fretted child lying upon it. He thought of the nights when he had cried himself to sleep, and of the mornings when he lay there weaving his fancies while a spider high above the window was spinning his web. There was the same old smell, and he sniffed the sorrow of his childhood.

"How long has this been here?" he asked.

"He was brought here about two weeks ago."

"I mean the bedstead. How long has it been in this corner?"

"Oh, I can't say as to that. I thought you meant the child. I've been here a long time, and I never saw the bedstead anywhere else. It will soon be thirty years since I came here. Do you care to go into any of the other rooms?"

"No, thank you."

They returned to the veranda. "Won't you sit down?" the old woman asked.

"No, I've but a few moments to stay. By the way, some time ago I met a man who said that he had lived here when a child. I was trying to think of his name. Oh, it was a man named Henry DeGolyer, I believe. Do you remember him?"

"Yes, but it was a long time ago. I heard somebody say that he lived in the city here, but he never came out to see us. Oh, yes, I remember him. He was a stupid little thing, but that didn't keep him from being mean. He oughtn't to have been taken in here, for he had a father."

"Did you know his father?"

"Who? John DeGolyer? I reckon I did, and he wa'n't no manner account, nuther. He had sense enough, but he throw himself away with liquor. He painted a picture of my youngest sister, and everybody said that it favored her mightily, but John wa'n't no manner account."

"Do you remember his wife?"

"Not much. He married a young creature down the river and broke her heart, folks said."

"Did you ever see her?"

His voice had suddenly changed, and the old woman looked sharply at him.

"Yes, several times. She was a tall, frail, black-eyed creature, and she might have done well if she hadn't ever met John DeGolyer. But won't you sit down?"

"No, thank you, I'm going now. You are the matron, I presume."

"Yes, sir—have been now for I hardly know how long."

"If I send some presents to the children will you see that they are properly distributed?"

"Yes, but for goodness' sake don't send any drums or horns."

"I won't. How many boys have you?"

"Well, we've got a good many, I can tell you. You see, this isn't a regular foundlings' home. We take up poor children from most, everywhere. We've got ninety-three boys."

And how many girls?"

"We've got a good many of them, too, I can tell you. Seventy-odd—seventy-five, I think."

"All right. Now don't forget your promise. Good day, madam."

He went to a large toy-shop and began to buy in a way that appeared likely to exhaust the stock.

"Where do you live?" asked the proprietor of the shop.

"In Chicago."

"What, you ain't going to ship these toys there and try to make anything on them, are you?"

"No; I want them sent out to the Foundlings' Home. What's your bill?"

The man figured up four hundred and ten dollars. "Come with me to the bank," said Henry.

"Nearly all you Chicago men are rich," remarked the toy merchant as they walked along. "I've had a notion to sell out and move there myself. Chicago's reaching out after everything, and New Orleans is doing more and more trading with her every year. I bought a good many of these toys from a Chicago drummer. He sells everything—represents a concern called the Colossus."

Henry settled for the toys, and then continued his stroll about the city. A strange sadness depressed him. The old woman's words—"and broke her heart, folks said"—rang in his ears. Had he been born as a mere incident of nature, or was it intended that he should achieve something? Was he an accident or was he designed? When he thought of his mother, his heart bled; but to think of his father made it beat with anger. When he became a member of the Witherspoon family, his conscience had constantly plied him with questions until, worn with self-argument, he resolved to accept a part of the advantages that were thrust upon him. Why not all? What sense had he shown in his obstinacy? What honor had he served? Why should he desire to reserve a part of a former self? Fortune had not favored his birth, but accident had thrown him in the way to be rich and therefore powerful. Accident! What could be more of an accident than life itself? Then came the last sting. The woman whom he loved, should she become his wife, would never know her name; his children—but how vain and foolish was such a questioning. Was his name worth preserving? Should he not rejoice in the thought that he had thrown it off? He stopped on a corner and stood in an old doorway, where he had blacked shoes. "George Witherspoon is right, and I have been a fool," he said. "Nature despises the weak. I will be rich—I am rich."

There was no half-heartedness now. His manner changed; there was arrogance in his step. Rich—powerful! The world had been his enemy and he had blacked its shoes. Now it should be his servant, and with a lordly contempt he would tip it for its services.

He turned into a restaurant, and in a masterful and overbearing way ordered his dinner. He looked at a man and mused: "He puts on airs, the fool! I could buy him."

Several men who had been sitting at a table got up to go out. One of them pointed at a ragged fellow who, some distance back, was down on his knees scrubbing the floor. "Zeb, see that man?"

"What man?"

"The one scrubbing the floor."

"That isn't a man—it's a thing. What of it?"

"Nothing, only he used to be one of the brightest newspaper writers in this city."

Henry looked up.

"Yes—used to write some great stuff, they say."

"What's his name?"

"Henry DeGolyer."

Henry sprang to his feet. He put out his hands, for the room began to swim round. He looked toward the door, but the men were gone. A waiter ran to him and caught him by the arm. "Sit down here, sir."

"No; get away."

He steadied himself against the wall. The ragged man looked
up, moved his bucket of water, dipped his mop-rag into it
and went on with his work. Henry took a stop forward, and
then felt for the wall again. A death-like paleness had
overspread his face, and he appeared vainly to be trying to
shut his staring and expressionless eyes. The waiter took
hold of his arm again.

"Never mind. I'm all right."

There were no customers in the room. The scrub-man came
nearer. Shudder after shudder, seeming to come in waves,
passed over Henry, but suddenly he became calm, and
slowly he walked toward the rear end of the room. The
scrub-man moved forward and was at Henry's feet. He
reached down and took hold of the man's arm—took the rag
out of his hand. The man looked up. There could be no
mistake. He was Henry Witherspoon.

"Don't you know me?" DeGolyer asked.

The man snatched the rag and began again to scrub the floor.

DeGolyer took hold of his arm. "Get up," he commanded,
and the man obeyed as if frightened.

"Don't you know me?"

"No."

"Don't you remember Hank?"

"I'm Hank," the man answered.

"No," said DeGolyer, with a sob, "you are Henry, and I am Hank."

"No, Henry's dead—I'm Hank." He dropped on his knees again and began to scrub the floor.

Just then the proprietor came in. "What's the trouble?" he asked. "Why, mister, don't pay any attention to that poor fellow. There's no harm in him."

"No one knows that better than I," DeGolyer answered. "How long has he been here—where did he come from?"

"He came off a ship. The cap'n said that he couldn't use him and asked me to take him. Been here about five months, I think. They say he used to amount to something, but he's gone up here," he added, tapping his head.

"What's the captain's name—where can I find him?"

"His ship's in now, I think. Go down to the levee and ask for the cap'n of the Creole."

"I will, but first let me tell you that I have come for this man. I know his father. I'll get back as soon as I can."

"All right. And if you can do anything for this poor fellow you are welcome to, for he's not much use round here."

DeGolyer snatched his hat and rushed out into the street. Not a hack was in sight; he could not wait for a car, and he hastened toward the river. He began to run, and a boy cried: "Sick him, Tige." He stopped suddenly and put his hand to his head. "Have I lost my mind?" he asked himself.

"Well, here we are again," some one said. DeGolyer looked

round and recognized the railroad man who had charge of the excursion.

"I'm glad I met you," DeGolyer replied. "It saves hunting you up."

"Why, what's the matter? Are you sick?"

"No, I'm all right, but something has occurred that compels me to return at once to Chicago."

"Nothing serious, I hope."

"No, but it demands my immediate return. I'm sorry, but it can't be helped. Good-by."

Again he started toward the river. He upset an old woman's basket of fruit. She cried out at him, and be saw that she could scarcely totter after the rolling oranges. He halted and picked them up for her. She mumbled something; she appeared to be a hundred years old. As he was putting the fruit into the basket, she struck a note in her mumbling that caused him to look her full in the face. He dropped the oranges and sprang back. She was the hag that had taken him from the Foundlings' Home. He hurried onward. "Great God!" he inwardly cried, "I am covered with the slime of the past."

Without difficulty he found the captain of the Creole. "I don't know very much about the poor fellow," he said. "I run across him nearly six months ago fit a little place called Dura, on the coast of Costa Rica. He was working about a sort of hotel, scrubbing and taking care of the horses; and I guess I shouldn't have paid any attention to him if I hadn't heard somebody say that he was an American; and it struck me as rather out of place that an American should be scrubbing round for those fellows, and I began to inquire about him. The landlord said that he was brought there sick, a good while ago, and was left for dead, but just as they were about to bury him he came to, and got up again after a few weeks. A priest told me that his name was Henry DeGolyer, and I said that it didn't make any difference what his name might be, I was going to take him back to the United States, so that if he had to clean out stables and scrub he might do it for white folks at least; for I am a down-east Yankee, and I haven't any too much respect for those fellows. Well, I brought him to New Orleans. I couldn't do much for him, being a poor man myself, but I got him a place in a restaurant, where he could get enough to eat, anyhow. I've since heard that he used to be a newspaper man, but this was disputed. Some people said that the newspaper DeGolyer was a black-haired fellow. But that didn't make any difference—I did the best I could."

"And you shall he more than paid for your trouble," said DeGolyer.

"Well, we won't argue about that. If you've got any money to spare you'd better give it to him."

"What is your name?"

"Atkins—just Cap'n Atkins."

"Where do you get your mail?"

"Well, I don't get any to speak of. A letter sent in care of the wharfmaster will reach me all right."

DeGolyer got into a hack and was rapidly driven to the restaurant. Young Witherspoon had completed his work and was in the kitchen, sitting on a box with a dirty-looking bundle lying beside him.

"Come, Henry," DeGolyer said, taking his arm.

"No; not Henry—Hank. Henry's dead."

"Come, my boy."

Witherspoon looked up, and closing his eyes, pressed the tips of his fingers against them.

"My boy."

"He got up and turned to go with DeGolyer, who held his arm, but perceiving that he had left his bundle, pulled back and made an effort to reach it.

"No, we don't want that," said DeGolyer.

"Yes, clothes."

"No, we'll get better clothes. Come on."

DeGolyer took him to a Turkish bath, to a barbershop, and then to a clothing store. It was now evening and nearly time to take the train for Chicago. They drove to the hotel and then to the railway station.

The homeward journey was begun, and the wheels kept on repeating: "A father and a mother and a sister, too." DeGolyer did not permit himself to think. His mind had a thousand quickenings, but he killed them. Young Witherspoon looked in awe at the luxury of the sleeping-car; he gazed at the floor as if he wondered how it could be scrubbed. At first he refused to sit on the showy plush, and even after DeGolyer's soothing and affectionate words had relieved his fear of giving offense, he jumped to his feet when the porter came through the car, and in a trembling fright begged his companion to protect him against the anger of the head waiter.

"Sit down, my dear boy. He is not a head waiter—he is your servant."

"Is he?"

"Yes, and must wait on you."

At this he doubtfully shook his head, and he continued to watch the porter until assured that he was not offended, and then timidly offered to shake hands with him.

When bed-time came young Witherspoon refused to take off his clothes. He was afraid that some one might steal them, and no argument served to reassure him; and even after he had lain down, with his clothes on, he took off a red neck-tie which he had insisted upon wearing, and for greater security put it into his pocket. DeGolyer lay beside him, and for a time Witherspoon was quiet, but suddenly he rose up and began to mutter.

"What's the matter, Henry?"

"Not Henry—Hank. Henry's dead."

"Well, what's the matter, Hank?"

"Want my hat."

"It's up there. We'll get it in the morning."

"Want it now."

DeGolyer got his hat for him, and he lay with it on his breast. How dragging a night it was! Would the train never run from under the darkness out into the light of day? And sometimes, when the train stopped, DeGolyer fancied that it had run ahead of night and perversely was waiting for the darkness to catch up. The end was coming, and what an end it might be!

The day was dark and rainy; the landscape was a flat dreariness. A buzzard flapped his heavy wings and flew from a dead tree; a yelping dog ran after the train; a horse, turned out to die, stumbled along a stumpy road.

It was evening when the train reached Chicago. DeGolyer and young Witherspoon took a cab and were driven to a hospital. The case was explained to the physician in charge. He said that the mental trouble might not be due to any permanent derangement of the brain; it was evident that he had not been treated properly. The patient's nervous system was badly shattered. The case was by no means hopeless. He could not determine the length of time it might require to restore him to physical health, which meant, he thought, a mental cure as well.

"Three months?" DeGolyer asked.

"That long, at least."

"I will leave him with you, and I urge you not to stop short of the highest medical skill that can be procured in either this country or in Europe. As to who this young man is or may turn out to be, that must be kept as a secret. I will call every day. Henry"—

"Hank."

"All right, Hank. Now, I'm going to leave you here, but I'll be back soon."

"No; they'll steal my clothes!" he cried, in alarm.

"No, they won't; they'll give you more clothes. You stay here, and I will bring you something when I come back."

DeGolyer went to a hotel.

CHAPTER XXXII

A MOST PECULIAR FELLOW

Early the next morning George Witherspoon was pacing the sidewalk in front of his house when DeGolyer came up. The merchant was startled.

"Why, where did you come from!" he exclaimed.

"I thought it best to get back as soon as possible," DeGolyer answered, shaking hands with him. "The truth is, I met a man who caused me to change my plans. He wants to buy my paper, and so I came back with him."

"Good enough, my dear boy. We'll go down immediately after breakfast and close with him one way or another. I am delighted, I assure you. Why, I missed you every minute of the time. See how I have already begun to rely on you? I haven't said a word to your mother about that angel. Hah, you'd burn down the Colossus, would you? Why, bless my life, you rascal."

"Who is that?" Ellen cried as they entered the hall; and with an airy, early-morning grace she came running down the stairway. "Oh, nobody can place any confidence in what you say," she declared, kissing him. "Goodness alive, man, you look as if you hadn't slept a wink since you left home." Just then Mrs. Witherspoon came out of the dining-room. "Mother," Ellen called, "here's one of your mother's people, and he's darker than ever."

Mrs. Witherspoon fondly kissed him before she gave Ellen the usual look of gentle reproach. "You must have known how much we missed you, my son, and that is the reason you came home. And you're just in time for breakfast. Ellen, *will* you please get out of the way? And what do you mean by saying that he's darker than ever?" Here she gave DeGolyer an anxious look. "But you are not ill, are you, my son?"

"Ill!" Witherspoon repeated, with resentment. "Of course he's not ill. What do you mean by ill? Do you expect a man to travel a thousand miles and then look like a rose? Is breakfast ready? Well, come then. We've got business to attend to."

"Now, as to this man who wants to buy my paper," said DeGolyer, when they were seated at the table, "let me tell you that he is a most peculiar fellow, and if he finds that I am anxious to sell, he'll back out. Therefore I don't think you'd better see him, father."

"Nonsense, my dear boy; I can make him buy in three minutes."

"That may be, but you might scare him off in one minute. He's an old-maidish sort of fellow, and is easily frightened. You'd better let me work him."

"All right, but don't haggle. There are transactions in which men are bettered by being beaten, and this is one of them."

"Yes, but it isn't well to let eagerness rush you into a folly."

"Ah, but in this affair folly was at the other end—at the buying."

"Then, with a wise sale, let us correct that folly."

"All right, but without haggling. When are you to meet this man again?"

"At noon."

"And when shall I see you?"

"Immediately after the deal is closed."

On DeGolyer's part the day was spent in the spinning of the threads of excuses. He might explain a week's delay, but how was he to account for a three months' put-off? And if at the end of that time young Witherspoon's case should be pronounced hopeless what course was then to be taken?

He did not see George Witherspoon again until dinner-time. The merchant met him with a quick inquiry. "We will discuss it in the library, father," DeGolyer answered.

"But can't you tell me now whether or not it has come out all right?"

"I think it's all right, but you may not. But let as wait until after dinner."

When they went into the library Witherspoon hastily lighted his cigar, and sat down in his leather-covered chair. "Well, how did it come out?" he asked.

DeGolyer did not sit down. Evidently he expected to remain in the room but a short time.

"I told you that he was a very peculiar fellow."

"Yes, I know that. What did you do with him?"

"Well, the deal isn't closed yet. He wants to go into the office and work three months before he decides."

"Tell him to go to the devil!" Witherspoon exclaimed.

"No, I can't do that."

"Why can't you? Do you belong to him? Have you a consideration for everybody but me?"

"I very nearly belong to him."

"You very nearly belong to him!" Witherspoon cried. "What in the name of God do you mean? Have you lost your senses?"

"My senses are all right, but my situation is peculiar."

"I should think so. Henry, I don't want to fly all to pieces. Lately, and with your help, I have pulled myself strongly together, and now I beg of you not to pull me apart."

"Father, some time ago you said that we have more control over ourselves than we exercise; and now I ask you to exert a little of that control. The sense of obligation has always been strong in me, and I feel that it is largely developed in you. I said that I very nearly belonged to this man, and I will tell you why; and don't be impatient, but listen to me for a few minutes. A number of years ago uncle left me in New Orleans and went on one of his trips to South America. He had not been gone long when yellow fever broke out. It was unusually fatal, and the city, though long accustomed to the disease, was panic-stricken. I was one of the early victims. Every member of the family I boarded with died within a week, and I was left in the house alone. This man, this peculiar fellow, Nat Parker, found me, took charge of me and did not leave me until I was out of danger. Of course, there was no way to reward him—you can merely stammer your gratitude to the man who has saved your life. He told me that the time might come when I could do him a good turn. Well, I met him the other day in New Orleans, and I incidentally spoke of my intention to sell my paper. He said that he would buy it. I told him that I would make him a present of it, but he resentfully replied that he was not a beggar. I came back with him to Chicago, and afraid that any interference might offend him, I told you that you should have nothing to do with the transaction. He has an ambition to become known as a newspaper man, and he foolishly believes that I am a great journalist. So he declares that for three months he must serve under me. What could I say? Could I tell him that I would dispose of the paper to some one else? I was compelled to accept his terms. I insisted that he should live with us during the time, but he objected. He swore that he must not be introduced to any of my people—to be petted like a dog that has saved a child's life. And there's the situation."

Witherspoon's cigar had fallen to the floor. Some time elapsed before he spoke, and when he did speak there was an unnatural softness in his voice. "Strange story," he said. "No wonder you are peculiar when you have been thrown among such peculiar people. If your friend were a sane man, we could deal with him in a sensible manner, but as he is not we must let him have his way. But suppose that at the end of three months he is tired of the paper?"

"I will sell it or give it away. But there'll be no trouble about that. It's a valuable piece of property, and I will swear to you that if at the end of that time Henry Witherspoon does not go into the Colossus with his father, it will be the father who keeps him out. Now promise me that you won't worry."

Witherspoon got up and took Henry's hand. "You have done the best you could, my son. It is peculiar and unbusinesslike, but we can't help that."

"Will you explain to mother?"

"Yes, but the more I look at it the stranger it seems. I don't know, however, that it is so strange after all. He is simply a chivalrous crank of the South, and we must humor him. But I'll be glad when all this nonsense is over."

DeGolyer sat in his room, smoking his pipe. He looked at his reflection in the mirror, and said: "Oh, what a liar you are! But your day for truth is coming."

CHAPTER XXXIII

THE TIME WAS DRAWING NEAR

One morning, when DeGolyer called at the hospital, young Witherspoon said to him: "You are Hank, and I'm Henry." And this was the first indication that his mind was regaining its health.

Every day George Witherspoon would ask: "Well, how's your peculiar friend getting along?" And one evening, when he made this inquiry, DeGolyer answered: "He is so much pleased that he doesn't think it will take him quite three months to decide."

"Good enough, but why doesn't he decide now?"

"Because it would hardly be in keeping with his peculiar methods. I haven't questioned him, but occasionally he drops a hint that leads me to believe that he's satisfied."

DeGolyer was once tempted to tell Richmond and McGlenn that he was feeling his way through a part that had been put upon him, but with this impulse came a restraining thought—the play was not yet done. They were at luncheon, and McGlenn had declared that DeGolyer was sometimes strangely inconsistent.

"I admit that I am, John, and with an explanation I could make you stare at me."

"Then let us have the explanation. Man was made to stare as well as to mourn."

"No, not now; but it will come one of these days, though perhaps not directly from me."

"Ah, you have killed a mysterious lion and made a riddle; but where is the honey you found in the carcass? Give us the explanation."

"Not now. But one of these bleak Chicago days you and Richmond will sit in the club, watch the whirling snow and discuss me, and you both will say that you always thought there was something strange about me."

"And we do," McGlenn replied. "Here's a millionaire's son, and he has chosen toil instead of ease. Isn't that an anomaly, and isn't such an anomaly a strange thing? But will the outcome of that vague something cause us to hold you at a cooler length from us—will that 'I told you so' result in your banishment? Shall we send a Roger Williams over the hills?"

"John, what are you trying to get at?" Richmond asked.

McGlenn looked serenely at him. "Have you devoured your usual quota of pickles? If so, writhe in your misery until I have dined."

"I writhe, not with what I have eaten, but at what I see. Is there a more distressing sight than an epicure—or a gourmand, rather—with a ragged purse?"

"Oh, yes; a stuffer, a glutton without a purse."

Richmond laughed. "Hunger may force a man to apparent gluttony," he said, "and a sandbagger may have taken his purse; and all on his part is honesty. But there is pretense—which I hold is not honest—in an effort to be an epicure."

"Ah, which you hold is not honest. A most rare but truthful avowal, since nothing you hold is honest."

"In my willingness to help the weak," Richmond replied, "I have held your overcoat while you put it on."

"And it was not an honest covering until you took your hands off."

"Neither did it cover honesty until some other man put it on by mistake," Richmond rejoined.

DeGolyer went to his office, and Richmond and McGlenn, wrangling as they walked along, betook themselves to the Press Club. "I tell you," said McGlenn, as they were going up the stairs, "that he needs our sympathy. He has suffered, but having suffered, he is great."

Thus the weeks were sprinkled with light incidents, and thus the days dripped into the past—and a designated future was drawing near.

"Well," Witherspoon remarked one Sunday morning, "the time set by your insane friend will soon be up."

"Yes, within a week," DeGolyer replied.

"I should think that he is more in need of apartments in an asylum than of a newspaper; but if he thinks he knows his business, all right; we have nothing to say. What has he agreed to give for the paper?"

"No price has been fixed, but there'll be no trouble about that."

"I hope not."

"Did you understand mother and Ellen to say they were going out shopping to-morrow afternoon?" DeGolyer asked.

"Yes, but what of it?"

"There's this of it: If they decide to go, I want you to meet me here at three o'clock."

"Why can't you meet me at the store?"

"Don't I tell you that my friend is peculiar?"

"Oh, it's to meet him, eh? All right, I'll be here."

His play was nearing the end. To-morrow he must snatch "the make-up" off his face. He felt a sadness that was more than half a joy. He should be free; he should be honest, and being honest, he could summon that most sterling of all strength, a manly self-respect. He had thought himself strong, but had found himself weak. The love of money, which at first had seemed so gross, at last had conquered him. This thought did not sting him now; it softened him, made him look with a more forgiving eye upon tempted human nature. But was it money that had tempted him to turn from a purpose so resolutely formed? Had not Witherspoon's argument and Ellen's persuasion left him determined to reserve one refuge for his mind—one closet wherein he could hang the cast-off garment of real self? Then it was the appeal of that gentle woman whom he called mother; it was not money. But after yielding to the mother he had found himself without a prop, and at last he had felt a contempt for a moderate income and had boasted to himself that he could buy a man. And for this he reproached himself. How grim was that something known as fate, how mockingly did it play with the children of men, and in that mockery how cold a justice! But he should be free, and that thought thrilled him.

In the afternoon he went over to the North Side, and along a modest street he walked, looking at the houses as if hunting for a number. He went up a short flight of wooden steps and rang the bell of the second flat. The hall door was open, and a moment later he saw Miss Drury at the head of the stairs.

"Why, is that you, Mr. Witherspoon?"

"Yes; may I come up?"

"What a question! Of course you may, especially as I am as lonesome as I can be."

He was shown into a neat sitting-room, where a canary bird "fluttered" his hanging cage up and down. A rose was pinned on one of the white curtains. The room was warmed by a stove, and through the isinglass the playful flame could be seen. She brought a "tidied" rocking-chair, and smiling in her welcome, said that as this was his first visit, she must make him comfortable. "Don't you see," she added, "that you constantly make me forget that I am working for you?"

"And don't you know," he answered, "that you are most pleasing when you do forget it? But I am to infer that you wouldn't give me the rocking-chair if you didn't forget that you were working for me?"

"You must infer nothing," she said. "But am I most pleasing when I forget? Then I will not remember again. It is a woman's duty to be pleasing; and her advantage, too, for when she ceases to please she loses many of her privileges."

DeGolyer went to the window, took the rose, brought it to her and said: "Put this in your hair."

She looked up as she took the rose; their eyes met and for a moment they lived in the promise of a delirious bliss. She looked down as she was putting the flower in her hair. He spoke an idle word that meant more than old Wisdom's speech, and she answered with a laugh that was nearly a sob. He thirsted to take her in his arms, to tell her of his love, but his time was not yet come—he was still Henry Witherspoon.

"How have you spent the day?" she asked.

"I'm thinking of to-morrow."

"And will to-morrow be so important?"

"Yes, the most important day of my life."

"Oh, tell me about it."

"I will to-morrow."

"Well, I suppose I shall have to wait, but I wish you would tell me just a little bit of it."

"To tell a little would be to tell all. The story is not yet complete."

"Oh, is it a story? And is it one that you are writing?"

"No, one that I am living. It is a strange tale."

"I know it must be interesting, but what has to-morrow to do with it?"

"It will be completed then."

"I don't understand you; I never did. I've often thought you the saddest man I have ever seen, and I've wondered why. You ought not to be sad—fortune is surely a friend of yours. You live in a grand house, and your father is a power in this great community. All the advantages of this life are within your reach; and if you can find cause to be sad, what must be the condition of people who have to struggle in order to live!"

"The summing-up of what you say means that I ought to be thankful."

"Yes, you were stolen, it is true, but you were restored, and therefore, by contrast and out of gratitude, you should be happier than if you had never been taken away."

"All that is true so far as it *is* true," he replied. "And let me say that I'm not so sad as you suppose. Do you care if I smoke here?"

"Not at all."

He lighted a cigar and sat smoking in silence. A boy shouted in the hall, a dog barked, and a cat sprang up from a doze under a table, looked toward the door, gave himself a humping stretch, and then lay down again.

Whenever DeGolyer looked at the girl, a new expression, the rosy tinge of a strange confusion, flew to her countenance. His talk evoked a self-possessed reply, but over his silence an embarrassment was brooding. She seemed to be in fear of something that sweetly she expected.

"I may not be at the office to-morrow until evening, but will you wait for me?"

"Yes."

"And when I come, I'll be myself."

"Be yourself? Who are you now?"

"Another man."

"Oh, then I shall be glad to see you."

"I don't know as to that. You may have strong objections to my real self."

"You are *so* mysterious."

"To-day, yes; to-morrow, no."

He was leaning back, blowing rings of smoke, and was looking up at them.

"Perhaps I shouldn't say it," she said, "but during the last three months you have appeared stranger than ever."

"Yes," he drawlingly replied, "for during the last three months it was natural that I should be stranger than ever."

"I do wish I knew what you mean."

"And when you have been told you may wish you had never known."

"Is it so bad as that?"

"Worse."

"Worse than what?"

"Than anything you imagine."

"Oh, you are simply trying to tease me, Mr. Witherspoon."

"Do you think so? Then we'll say no more about it."

"Oh, but that's worse than ever. Well, I don't care; I can wait."

They talked on subjects in which neither of them was interested, but sympathy was in their voices. Gradually— yes, now it seemed for months—they had been floating toward that fern-covered island in the river of life where a thoughtless word comes back with an echo of love; where the tongue may be silly, but where the eye holds a redeemed soul, returned from God to gaze upon the only remembered rapture of this earth.

She went with him to the head of the stairway. "Don't leave the office before I come," he called, looking back at her.

"You know I won't," she answered.

CHAPTER XXXIV

TOLD HIM A STORY

At the appointed time, the next day, George Witherspoon was waiting in his library. DeGolyer came in a cab, and when he got out, he told the driver to wait.

"Where is your friend?" Witherspoon asked as DeGolyer entered the room.

"He'll be here within a few minutes."

"Confound him, I'm getting sick of his peculiarities."

The merchant sat down; DeGolyer stood on the hearth-rug. The time was come, and he had been strong, but now a shiver crept over him.

"My friend told me a singular story to-day."

"I don't doubt it; and if his stories are as singular as he is, they must he marvelous."

"This story *is* marvelous, and I think it would interest you. I will give it to you briefly. There were two young men in a foreign country"—

"I wish he was in a foreign country. I can't wait here all day."

"He'll be here soon. These two friends were on their way to the sea coast, and here's where it will strike you. One of them had been stolen when he was a child, and was now going back to his parents. But before they reached the coast, the rich man's son—as we'll call the one who had been stolen—was stricken with a fever. No ship was in port, and his friend took him to a hotel and got a doctor for him."

"Wish you'd hand me a match," said Witherspoon. "My cigar's out. Thank you."

"Got a doctor for him, but he grew worse. Sometimes he was delirious, but at times his mind was strangely clear; and once, when he was rational, he told his friend that he was going to die. He didn't appear to care very much so far as it concerned himself, but the thought of the grief that his death would cause his parents seemed to lie as a cold weight upon his mind. And it was then that he made a most peculiar request. He compelled his friend to promise to take his name; to go to his home; to be a son to his father and mother. His friend begged, but had to yield. Well, the rich man's son died, we'll suppose, and the poor fellow took his name on the spot. He had to leave hurriedly, for a father and a mother and a sister were waiting in a distant home. A ship that had just come was ready to sail, and a month might pass before the landing of another vessel. He went to these people as their son"—

"Oh, yes," said Witherspoon, "and fell in love with the sister, and then had to tell his story."

"No, he didn't. He loved the girl, but only as a brother should. He was not wholly acceptable to his father, but"—

"Ah, that's all very well," said Witherspoon, "but what proof had he?"

DeGolyer met Witherspoon's careless look and held it with a firm gaze. And slowly raising his hand, he said: "He held up a gold chain."

Witherspoon sprang to his feet and exclaimed: "My God, he's crazy!"

"Wait!"

The merchant had turned toward the door. He halted and looked back.

"George Witherspoon"—

"I thought so—crazy. Merciful God, he's mad!"

"Will you listen to me for a moment—just a moment—and I will prove to you that I'm not crazy. I am not your son—my name is Henry DeGolyer. Wait, I tell you!" Witherspoon had staggered against the door-case. "I am not your son, but your son is not dead. I took his place; I thought it a promise made to a dying man."

"What!" he whispered. His voice was gone. "You—you"—

DeGolyer ran to him and eased him into his chair. "Your son is here, and the man who has brought nothing but ill luck will leave you. I tried to soften this, but couldn't," Witherspoon's head shook as he looked up at him. "Wait a moment, and I will call him. No, don't get up."

DeGolyer hastened to the front door, and standing on the steps, he called: "Henry! oh, Henry!"

"All right, Hank."

Young Witherspoon got out of the cab and came up the steps.

"He is waiting for you, Henry." And speaking to the footman, DeGolyer added: "There's nothing the matter. Send those girls about their business."

Young Witherspoon followed DeGolyer into the library. The merchant was standing with his shaky hands on the back of a chair. He stepped forward and tried to speak, but failed.

"I'm your son. Hank did as I told him. It's all right. I've had a fever—he's going to fall, Hank!"

They eased him down into his leather-covered chair.

"I see it now," the old man muttered. "Yes, I can see it. Come here."

The young man leaned over and put his arms about his father's neck. "I will go into the store with you when I get just a little stronger—I will do anything you want me to. I've had an awful time—awful—but it's all right now. Hank found me in New Orleans, scrubbing a floor; but it's all right now."

"I'll get him some brandy," said DeGolyer.

"No," Witherspoon objected, "I'll be myself in a minute. Never was so shocked in my life. Who ever heard of such a thing? Of course you couldn't soften it. Let me look at you, my son. How do I know what to believe? No, there's no mistake now."

He got up, and holding the young man's hands, stood looking at him. "Who's that?" he asked.

They heard voices. Mrs. Witherspoon and Ellen were coming down the hall. DeGolyer stepped hastily to the door.

"Oh, what are you doing here?" Ellen cried. "I saw some-body—Miss Miller. She didn't say so, but I know that she wants me to kiss you for her, and I will."

"Ellen!" Witherspoon exclaimed, and just then she saw that a stranger was present.

"Excuse me," she said.

DeGolyer took her by the hand, and as Mrs. Witherspoon came up he held out his other hand to her. He led them both to the threshold of the library, gently drew them into the room, and quickly stepping out, closed the door and hastened upstairs.

As he entered his room he thought that he heard a cry, and he listened, but naught save a throbbing silence came from below. He sat down, put his arms on the table, and his head lay an aching weight upon his arms. After a time he got up, and taking his traveling-bag from a closet, began to pack it. There was his old pipe, still with a ribbon tied about the stem. He waited a long time and then went down-stairs. The library door was closed, and gently he rapped upon it. Witherspoon's voice bade him enter.

Mrs. Witherspoon was sitting on a sofa; young Henry was on his knees, and his head was in her lap. Witherspoon and Ellen were standing near.

"He is like my father's people," the mother said, fondly

stroking his hair. "All the Springers were light." She looked at DeGolyer, and her eyes were soft, but for him they no longer held the glow of a mother's love. DeGolyer put down his bag near the door.

"Mr. Witherspoon, I hardly know what to say. I came to this house as a lie, but I shall leave it as a truth. I"—

"Hank!" young Henry cried, getting up, "you ain't going away. You are going to stay here."

He ran to DeGolyer, seized his hand, and leading him to Ellen, said: "I have caught you a prince. Take him." And DeGolyer, smiling sadly, replied, "I love her as a brother." She held out her hands to him. "I could never think of you as anything else," she said.

"But you must not leave us," Mrs. Witherspoon declared, coming forward.

"Yes, my mission here is ended."

"You shan't go, Hank," young Witherspoon cried.

"Henry," said DeGolyer, "I did as you requested. Now it is your time to obey. Keep quiet!" He stood erect; he had the bearing of a master. He turned to Witherspoon. "Here is a check for the amount of money you advanced me, with interest added."

Witherspoon stepped back. "I refuse to take it," he said.

"But you *shall* take it. I have sold the paper at a profit, and it has made money almost from the first. Do as I tell you. Take this check."

The merchant took the check, and it shook in his hand. DeGolyer now addressed Mrs. Witherspoon. "You have indeed been a mother to me. No gentler being ever lived, and till the day of my death I shall remember you with affection."

"Oh, this is all so strange!" she cried, weeping.

"Yes, but everything is strange, when we come to think of it. God bless you. Sister,"—Ellen gave him her hands,—"good-by."

He kissed the girl, and then kissed Mrs. Witherspoon. Henry came toward him, but DeGolyer stopped him with a wave of his hand. "My dear boy, I'm not going out of the world. No, you mustn't grab hold of me. Stand where you are. You shall hear from me. Mr. Witherspoon, this time you must get up a statement without my help—I mean for the newspapers. I know that I have caused you a great deal of worry, but it is a pretty hard matter to live a lie even when it is imposed as a duty. By the way, a poor sea captain, Atkins is his name, brought Henry from Dura. I wish you would send him a check, care Wharfmaster, New Orleans."

"I will."

"Good-by, Mr. Witherspoon."

"Henry DeGolyer," said Witherspoon, grasping his hand, "you are the most honorable man I ever met."

"There, now!" DeGolyer cried, holding up his hand—they all were coming toward him—"do as I tell you and remain where you are."

He caught up his bag and hastened out. "To the *Star* office," he said to the cabman.

CHAPTER XXXV

CONCLUSION

"I'd began to think that you'd forgotten to come," said Miss Drury, as DeGolyer entered the room. She was sitting at her desk, and hits of torn paper were scattered about her.

"I'm sorry that I kept you waiting so long," he replied. He did not sit down, but stood near her.

"Oh, it hasn't been so *very* long," she rejoined. "Why, how you have changed since yesterday," she added, looking at him.

"For the worse?" he asked.

"For the better; you look more like the heir to a great fortune."

He smiled. "I am an heir to freedom, and that is the greatest of fortune."

"Oh, now you are trying to mystify me again; and you said that to-day you would make everything clear."

"And I shall. Laura"—she looked up quickly—he repeated,

"this is my last day in this office. I have sold the paper, and the new owner will take charge to-morrow."

"I'm sorry," she said, and then added: "But on my part that is selfishness. Of course you know what is best for yourself."

"I told you yesterday that my story would be completed to-day. It is, and I will tell it."

The latest edition had left the press, and there was scarcely a sound in the building. The sharp cry of the newsboy came from the street.

In telling her his story be did not begin with his early life, but with the time when first he met young Witherspoon. It was a swift recital; and he sought not to surprise her; he strove to tone down her amazement.

"And to-day I took his son to him. I saw the quick transfer of a mother's love and of a father's interest—I saw a girl half-frightened at the thought that upon a stranger she had bestowed the intimacies of a sister's affection. I had made so strong an effort to be honorable with myself, at least; to persuade myself that I was fulfilling an honest mission, but had failed, for at last I had fallen to the level of an ordinary hypocrite; I had found myself to be a purse-proud fool. When I went into that restaurant my sympathies were dead, and when that man pointed at the poor menial and said that his name was Henry DeGolyer"—

"No, no," she said, hiding her face, "your sympathies were not dead. You—you were a hero."

"I was simply a frozen-blooded fool," he replied. "And now I must tell you something, but I know that it will make you despise me. My father was a beast—he broke my mother's heart. The first thing I remember, her dead arms were about me and a chill was upon me—I knew not the meaning of death, but I was terrorized by its cold mystery. I cried out, but no one came, and there in the dark, with that icy problem, I remained alone"—

"Oh, don't," she cried, and her hands seemed to flutter in her lap. She got up, and putting her arms on the top of the desk, leaned her head upon them.

"How could I despise you for that?" she sobbed.

"Not for that," he bitterly answered, "but for this I was taken to the Foundlings' Home—was taken from that place to become the disgraceful property of an Italian hag. She taught me, compelled me to be a thief. Once she and some ruffians robbed a store and forced me to help them. I ought to have died before that. She demanded that I should steal something every day, and if I didn't she beat me. I got up early one morning and robbed *her*. I took a handful of money out of her drawer and ran away. But in the street a horror seized me, and I threw the money in the gutter and fled from it. Don't you see that I was born a thief? But I have striven so hard since then to be an honorable man. But don't try not to pity, to despise me. You can't help it. But, my God, I do love you!"

She turned toward him with a glory in her eyes, and he caught her in his arms.

The old building was silent, and the shout of the newsboy was far away.

"Angel of sweet mercy," he said, still holding her in his arms, "let us leave this struggling place. I know of an old house in Virginia—it is near the sea, and rest lies in the woods about it. Let us live there, not to dream idly, but to work, to be a devoted man and his happy wife. Come."

He took her hand, and they went out into the hall. The place was deserted, the elevator was not running, and down the dark stairway he led her—out into the light of the street.

THE END

Opie Read

Choose from Thousands of 1stWorldLibrary Classics By

A. M. Barnard
Ada Leverson
Adolphus William Ward
Aesop
Agatha Christie
Alexander Aaronsohn
Alexander Kielland
Alexandre Dumas
Alfred Gatty
Alfred Ollivant
Alice Duer Miller
Alice Turner Curtis
Alice Dunbar
Allen Chapman
Alleyne Ireland
Ambrose Bierce
Amelia E. Barr
Amory H. Bradford
Andrew Lang
Andrew McFarland Davis
Andy Adams
Angela Brazil
Anna Alice Chapin
Anna Sewell
Annie Besant
Annie Hamilton Donnell
Annie Payson Call
Annie Roe Carr
Annonaymous
Anton Chekhov
Archibald Lee Fletcher
Arnold Bennett
Arthur C. Benson
Arthur Conan Doyle
Arthur M. Winfield
Arthur Ransome
Arthur Schnitzler
Arthur Train
Atticus
B.H. Baden-Powell
B. M. Bower
B. C. Chatterjee
Baroness Emmuska Orczy
Baroness Orczy
Basil King
Bayard Taylor
Ben Macomber
Bertha Muzzy Bower
Bjornstjerne Bjornson

Booth Tarkington
Boyd Cable
Bram Stoker
C. Collodi
C. E. Orr
C. M. Ingleby
Carolyn Wells
Catherine Parr Traill
Charles A. Eastman
Charles Amory Beach
Charles Dickens
Charles Dudley Warner
Charles Farrar Browne
Charles Ives
Charles Kingsley
Charles Klein
Charles Hanson Towne
Charles Lathrop Pack
Charles Romyn Dake
Charles Whibley
Charles Willing Beale
Charlotte M. Braeme
Charlotte M. Yonge
Charlotte Perkins Stetson
Clair W. Hayes
Clarence Day Jr.
Clarence E. Mulford
Clemence Housman
Confucius
Coningsby Dawson
Cornelis DeWitt Wilcox
Cyril Burleigh
D. H. Lawrence
Daniel Defoe
David Garnett
Dinah Craik
Don Carlos Janes
Donald Keyhoe
Dorothy Kilner
Dougan Clark
Douglas Fairbanks
E. Nesbit
E. P. Roe
E. Phillips Oppenheim
E. S. Brooks
Earl Barnes
Edgar Rice Burroughs
Edith Van Dyne
Edith Wharton

Edward Everett Hale
Edward J. O'Biren
Edward S. Ellis
Edwin L. Arnold
Eleanor Atkins
Eleanor Hallowell Abbott
Eliot Gregory
Elizabeth Gaskell
Elizabeth McCracken
Elizabeth Von Arnim
Ellem Key
Emerson Hough
Emilie F. Carlen
Emily Bronte
Emily Dickinson
Enid Bagnold
Enilor Macartney Lane
Erasmus W. Jones
Ernie Howard Pie
Ethel May Dell
Ethel Turner
Ethel Watts Mumford
Eugene Sue
Eugenie Foa
Eugene Wood
Eustace Hale Ball
Evelyn Everett-green
Everard Cotes
F. H. Cheley
F. J. Cross
F. Marion Crawford
Fannie E. Newberry
Federick Austin Ogg
Ferdinand Ossendowski
Fergus Hume
Florence A. Kilpatrick
Fremont B. Deering
Francis Bacon
Francis Darwin
Frances Hodgson Burnett
Frances Parkinson Keyes
Frank Gee Patchin
Frank Harris
Frank Jewett Mather
Frank L. Packard
Frank V. Webster
Frederic Stewart Isham
Frederick Trevor Hill
Frederick Winslow Taylor

Friedrich Kerst
Friedrich Nietzsche
Fyodor Dostoyevsky
G.A. Henty
G.K. Chesterton
Gabrielle E. Jackson
Garrett P. Serviss
Gaston Leroux
George A. Warren
George Ade
Geroge Bernard Shaw
George Cary Eggleston
George Durston
George Ebers
George Eliot
George Gissing
George MacDonald
George Meredith
George Orwell
George Sylvester Viereck
George Tucker
George W. Cable
George Wharton James
Gertrude Atherton
Gordon Casserly
Grace E. King
Grace Gallatin
Grace Greenwood
Grant Allen
Guillermo A. Sherwell
Gulielma Zollinger
Gustav Flaubert
H. A. Cody
H. B. Irving
H.C. Bailey
H. G. Wells
H. H. Munro
H. Irving Hancock
H. R. Naylor
H. Rider Haggard
H. W. C. Davis
Haldeman Julius
Hall Caine
Hamilton Wright Mabie
Hans Christian Andersen
Harold Avery
Harold McGrath
Harriet Beecher Stowe
Harry Castlemon
Harry Coghill
Harry Houidini

Hayden Carruth
Helent Hunt Jackson
Helen Nicolay
Hendrik Conscience
Hendy David Thoreau
Henri Barbusse
Henrik Ibsen
Henry Adams
Henry Ford
Henry Frost
Henry James
Henry Jones Ford
Henry Seton Merriman
Henry W Longfellow
Herbert A. Giles
Herbert Carter
Herbert N. Casson
Herman Hesse
Hildegard G. Frey
Homer
Honore De Balzac
Horace B. Day
Horace Walpole
Horatio Alger Jr.
Howard Pyle
Howard R. Garis
Hugh Lofting
Hugh Walpole
Humphry Ward
Ian Maclaren
Inez Haynes Gillmore
Irving Bacheller
Isabel Cecilia Williams
Isabel Hornibrook
Israel Abrahams
Ivan Turgenev
J.G.Austin
J. Henri Fabre
J. M. Barrie
J. M. Walsh
J. Macdonald Oxley
J. R. Miller
J. S. Fletcher
J. S. Knowles
J. Storer Clouston
J. W. Duffield
Jack London
Jacob Abbott
James Allen
James Andrews
James Baldwin

James Branch Cabell
James DeMille
James Joyce
James Lane Allen
James Lane Allen
James Oliver Curwood
James Oppenheim
James Otis
James R. Driscoll
Jane Abbott
Jane Austen
Jane L. Stewart
Janet Aldridge
Jens Peter Jacobsen
Jerome K. Jerome
Jessie Graham Flower
John Buchan
John Burroughs
John Cournos
John F. Kennedy
John Gay
John Glasworthy
John Habberton
John Joy Bell
John Kendrick Bangs
John Milton
John Philip Sousa
John Taintor Foote
Jonas Lauritz Idemil Lie
Jonathan Swift
Joseph A. Altsheler
Joseph Carey
Joseph Conrad
Joseph E. Badger Jr
Joseph Hergesheimer
Joseph Jacobs
Jules Vernes
Julian Hawthrone
Julie A Lippmann
Justin Huntly McCarthy
Kakuzo Okakura
Karle Wilson Baker
Kate Chopin
Kenneth Grahame
Kenneth McGaffey
Kate Langley Bosher
Kate Langley Bosher
Katherine Cecil Thurston
Katherine Stokes
L. A. Abbot
L. T. Meade

L. Frank Baum
Latta Griswold
Laura Dent Crane
Laura Lee Hope
Laurence Housman
Lawrence Beasley
Leo Tolstoy
Leonid Andreyev
Lewis Carroll
Lewis Sperry Chafer
Lilian Bell
Lloyd Osbourne
Louis Hughes
Louis Joseph Vance
Louis Tracy
Louisa May Alcott
Lucy Fitch Perkins
Lucy Maud Montgomery
Luther Benson
Lydia Miller Middleton
Lyndon Orr
M. Corvus
M. H. Adams
Margaret E. Sangster
Margret Howth
Margaret Vandercook
Margaret W. Hungerford
Margret Penrose
Maria Edgeworth
Maria Thompson Daviess
Mariano Azuela
Marion Polk Angellotti
Mark Overton
Mark Twain
Mary Austin
Mary Catherine Crowley
Mary Cole
Mary Hastings Bradley
Mary Roberts Rinehart
Mary Rowlandson
M. Wollstonecraft Shelley
Maud Lindsay
Max Beerbohm
Myra Kelly
Nathaniel Hawthrone
Nicolo Machiavelli
O. F. Walton
Oscar Wilde
Owen Johnson
P.G. Wodehouse
Paul and Mabel Thorne

Paul G. Tomlinson
Paul Severing
Percy Brebner
Percy Keese Fitzhugh
Peter B. Kyne
Plato
Quincy Allen
R. Derby Holmes
R. L. Stevenson
R. S. Ball
Rabindranath Tagore
Rahul Alvares
Ralph Bonehill
Ralph Henry Barbour
Ralph Victor
Ralph Waldo Emmerson
Rene Descartes
Ray Cummings
Rex Beach
Rex E. Beach
Richard Harding Davis
Richard Jefferies
Richard Le Gallienne
Robert Barr
Robert Frost
Robert Gordon Anderson
Robert L. Drake
Robert Lansing
Robert Lynd
Robert Michael Ballantyne
Robert W. Chambers
Rosa Nouchette Carey
Rudyard Kipling
Saint Augustine
Samuel B. Allison
Samuel Hopkins Adams
Sarah Bernhardt
Sarah C. Hallowell
Selma Lagerlof
Sherwood Anderson
Sigmund Freud
Standish O'Grady
Stanley Weyman
Stella Benson
Stella M. Francis
Stephen Crane
Stewart Edward White
Stijn Streuvels
Swami Abhedananda
Swami Parmananda
T. S. Ackland

T. S. Arthur
The Princess Der Ling
Thomas A. Janvier
Thomas A Kempis
Thomas Anderton
Thomas Bailey Aldrich
Thomas Bulfinch
Thomas De Quincey
Thomas Dixon
Thomas H. Huxley
Thomas Hardy
Thomas More
Thornton W. Burgess
U. S. Grant
Upton Sinclair
Valentine Williams
Various Authors
Vaughan Kester
Victor Appleton
Victor G. Durham
Victoria Cross
Virginia Woolf
Wadsworth Camp
Walter Camp
Walter Scott
Washington Irving
Wilbur Lawton
Wilkie Collins
Willa Cather
Willard F. Baker
William Dean Howells
William le Queux
W. Makepeace Thackeray
William W. Walter
William Shakespeare
Winston Churchill
Yei Theodora Ozaki
Yogi Ramacharaka
Young E. Allison
Zane Grey

www.ingramcontent.com/pod-product-compliance
Lightning Source LLC
Chambersburg PA
CBHW020816260626
47169CB00003B/695